I0745686

ALMOST TOMORROW

Sean Mcquade

Almost Tomorrow is a riveting story of two sisters, Parveen and Bulbul and their journey to survival. The book, to begin with, tackles so much that history, speaking of publication—has not been given much attention to. As such is the Brick-Kiln industry in Pakistan which bonded Parveen and the other young people as a result of landlessness and high unemployment. They were all compelled to take money in advance from kiln owners for their daily sustenance by selling their labor. Further, this book digs deep into what transpired between Pakistan and India after the World War II took place. Also, this book would raise questions whether or not Great Britain was indeed good for India and its people, considering that their steps were evident.

Although written in a fictitious manner, this book by Sean Mcquade is a beautiful literary piece and an informative one which gives every reader, especially the younger generation a clear picture of Anglo Indians and their community's contribution to the country. The chapters are dealt concisely with photos to illustrate the text and I find it to be a writing that is well crossed-referenced.

I would not say this book is for all since the history and its recipe can only get complicated somewhere in the story, but any good reader will definitely love this book and the heart that has been put to it by the author and any reader can totally feel it. *Almost Tomorrow* is a book that pictures struggles, sacrifices and hope—a highly commendable book!

—Nova Cage PA Book Review

Introduction

Even though this book, *Almost Tomorrow*, is based upon the life story of an Anglo-Indian lady from Goa, pre-partition of India oriented around 1947 and there afterwards includes tales of the lives of her extended family.

Parveen and her younger sister Bulbul had, through no fault of their own, ended up trapped for life as bonded laborers in the brick-kiln industry in Pakistan.

Their drama began at an early age when their family moved from Goa to a small railway town called Kamoke situated in rural Punjab. The years just after World War 2, the partition of the Indian subcontinent and the formation of Pakistan and India as separate independent nations came into being. An account of one single massacre in the Kamoke railway station provides the reader with a window into what might possibly have happened to a portion of approximately 1.5 million people who were murdered or killed during the mayhem.

Also, that year, the mighty British Raj was preparing to finalize their occupation of the Indian subcontinent and return to Great Britain. They had repulsed a Japanese massive attempt to invade Northeast India from Burma. The British army, along with the support of a couple of Indian regiments and American air support, suppressed the advance.

One of Lord Louis Mountbatten's chief contribution was to coordinate the partition on behalf of Her Majesty Queen Elizabeth. He also was responsible for drawing up the new international (Radcliffe Line) boundary between the two new countries. The agreement went ahead on 14–15 August 1947 in the company of Prime Minister Nehru representing India and Jinnah, the 'Quaid-E-Azam' (Founder of the Nation), representing Pakistan.

The story began in the 80s. Praveen, at the time was a grandmother, shared her stories with a group of workers at the end of their hard day's work in the clay pits, brick kiln, and farmlands.

As the sun sank low in the skies, out across the semi-arid desert, one could not but notice how, at forty-eight, Parveen looked much older than her age because of the harsh climate and her individual lifelong struggle for survival. Nothing much had changed in their lives since she and Bulbul were transported to live in the desert. This was where they learnt to face up to the various issues because of inadequate health facilities, and lack of basic infrastructure. Regular droughts, famines, infant mortality, malaria, and waterborne diseases were a commonplace reality. Imran, her grandson, and his new-found friend Tariq were supposedly kidnapped by a syndicate of people smugglers before they had been shipped off overseas to the United Arab Emirates to participate in wild camel races to entertain the wealthier elements of that society and the international expatriate community. The kidnappers spent eight months training the boys and few other kids in the art of camel riding, camel racing, and basic Arabic and Middle Eastern customs.

After a full year of verbal abuse and physical exhaustion. The Pakistani minder helped the two boys Imran and Tariq, escape from the United Arab Emirates and return by ship to Pakistan.

Okay, it was not over yet. The boys found themselves struggling to survive in a dangerous harsh environment called *Baluchistan*, long before a group of Afghan Nomads (Kuchi's) came to notice them. The leader brought them to their encampment, and he eventually adopted the boys to look after goats and camels in the mountains bordering *Afghanistan*.

At the time, the *Russians* were at war in Afghanistan, the nomads (Kuchi's) earned vast amounts of money by smuggling American supplies of weapons and ammunitions across the mountains bordering Pakistan and Afghanistan to supply the fighters of the rebellion.

As the boys entered their early teens, they became a part of one of these caravans of camel herders transporting weapons and supplies across the border into Afghanistan… so be it! *Their strong desire to survive and unwanted adventure and misfortune continued.*

Deep inside, Parveen carried the burden of selling off her seven-year-old grandson. Did he mysteriously disappear at Christian Christmas celebrations? However, Praveen went to her grave never knowing whatever happened to him. She was certain he would have made his life better than the miserable one he was enduring within the brick-kiln community.

Parveen is a name commonly given to girls but can be a boy's name too. It is stated that it derives from Persia and India.

Pleiades is the seven sisters' cluster or group of stars in the galaxy.

It is said that people with the name have a naturally deep inner desire to inspire people to develop themselves to serve in a higher cause. They also instinctively have the desire to openly share their own views on spiritual matters at the drop of a hat.

People with this name tend to be affectionate, compassionate, intuitive, humanitarian, broadminded, generous with a big heart, romantic and usually have very energetic and dynamic personalities.

When given an opportunity, they are keen to orientate into services where they can serve in humanitarian organizations.

Because of their openness, they are easily led, exploited, or imposed upon.

About the Author

McQuade was born in 1954 in Dublin. His parents are originally from Belfast. He has always considered himself to be Northern Irish. He has an extensive employment background, having travelled around the world, from Ireland to Australia, and having joined the Irish army. The Corps of Engineers also provided professional military services on active duties on the border with Northern Ireland, United Nations peacekeeping in Southern Lebanon, and humanitarian technical engineering support in Pakistan, Afghanistan, and Nuristan. He could speak some Arabic, Punjabi, and Urdu. He lived in Lahore and got married to Grace Natta Lotto in 1986. His son Martin was born the following year in Gulberg, Lahore. He is now a grandad of two fine children—Keira and Callan.

Other Publications

Our Fathers' Fate was published by Xlibris in the USA, UK, and Australia in 2015, an autobiography consisting of 286 pages, available online on Amazon, Xlibris, and Barnes & Noble in e-book, paperback, and hardcover types.

Our Fathers' Fate was exhibited at the 2016 Frankfurt Book Fair, proudly representing Australian writers in the self-publishing section.

In a brick kiln, Thar Desert, Sindh Province, Pakistan...

The Thar Desert felt hotter than usual for that time of the year. Normally, it has a semi-arid climate where April, May, and June are some of the hottest months of the year. It was stated that temperatures reached up to forty-five degrees during the day and hovered around as high as thirty degrees overnight.

During the day in the winter months, if one is walking through the desert, facing the sun, the front of the body feels warmer, and the back facing away will feel much colder.

The sand is so fine in places resembling talcum powder that can enter every orifice of one's body.

May 1980

As evening fell across the semi-arid desert where the landscape was harsh and unforgettable, the extraordinary, hard, monotonous day had finished for the little community of workers who had been working under a blistering sunny day in the brick kilns and pits, along with a group of brick kiln and another group of laborers from the sugarcane fields.

As usual, the workers—mainly women and children—had gathered around the small waterfall generated from an agricultural water-irrigation channel that flowed from high up the hill as they were taking turns to wash the caked mud from their bodies under the falling water.

THE ASSEMBLY BEGINS TO GATHER

As Parveen, she attempted to get up from where she had been bent over all day, moulding bricks.

Even though she was tired, she waved, smiled, and greeted each one as she wobbled along to make her way up across the darkness of the pit to join with the rest of the bonded laborers. Most of the group were sitting patiently in line, awaiting turns to wash.

Parveen was one of the older ladies. Usually, they could wash themselves first. But this evening, as she approached a clearing to dry her hair, a much younger lady made way as a sign of respect for her elders. She signalled to her and instantly moved to the side to let her pass by. 'Hello, Auntie,' said one of the other young women and ventured to enquire in an inquisitive type of way.

'Well then, Aunty Parveen, can I ask you, how did you, a Punjabi lady, manage to end up down here? How come you are working and living here in the Thar Desert and not up there on the fertile flat plains of the Punjab where you belong?'

Parveen looked down at a line of marching ants passing over her tiny feet. She leaned down to swipe them away. Beforehand, she scratched her forehead and swiped a fly away from her face. During these actions, she scanned and scrutinized the rest of the people in the assembly area and said, 'Well, you know that is a very long story. I feel that I might upset some finer people here with the content. Therefore, I'd prefer to refrain from telling you anything about my past life. There are parts of my life I would like to forget and other parts I cherish to deeply to talk about in public.'

The evening sun shining on her face really showed her age. Wrinkles etched deep around her eyes, and two inches growth of grey roots on her long, shoulder-length henna-dyed reddish hair.

PARVEEN

She looked elegant with her precious piece of gold in her nose piercing and an arm full of multi-colored bangles stretching all the way up her right arm to the elbow—a familiar fashion and traditional custom of the Sindh womenfolk.

She had adapted since her arrival to work and lived here in the desert. Parveen's face portrayed an expression of humbleness and simplicity.

She had adapted since her arrival to work and lived here in the desert. Parveen's face portrayed an expression of humbleness and simplicity. Dressed in her light blue kameez pants covered in brown mud, the cloth almost treading bear at the knees, she moved elegantly as she slowly lowered her pain-riddled body to sit on the edge of a pile of bricks. She spoke softly but with a posture of a person of stature. She began to speak. 'As you know, my life is just going okay for me. I am happy to be living amongst you, fine friends and neighbors.

'I am a bit apprehensive to disclose my journey in through my harsh existence of life before. I would really prefer to leave it behind me. So I really do not wish to attract any attention or trouble on myself or on my family. But I am sure too that my story would not be of interest to most of you as you too have your own hardship stories to tell on how you all ended up here. Moreover, I'm sure you all have much to do at home for your husbands and families. So I'm sure you do not have the time to listen to my boring story.'

'Please, Parveen! We want you to tell us now. Isn't that, right?' said one of ladies in the assembly as she glanced around to seek the approval of the other people present.

'Oh yes! Please tell us,' they started chanting in harmony.

'Okay then,' she replied. 'Can someone go and put the kettle on the kiln?' Most of the workers used the kiln to boil water for washing, cooking food, and making tea.

I believe we are going to be here for a long time, she thought. *Also, maybe it's because of the heavy, depressing humidity and atmosphere here in Sindh that all those dried-up wells and the silence of the desert, with its shifting whispering sands, seems to be making me feel homesick for the Punjab. Yeah, really, it's a hard place to be after knowing a better life in my past level on this planet the of a life in the Punjab.*

KIDS PLAYING CRICKET BELOW THE SAND DUNES

Looking around as a group, some of them pulled up some charpoy beds to sit on, while others prepared a couple of oil lanterns to light up the area as night-time was setting in. They settled in to the sounds of a howling dog, a crowing hen, and the clatter of ball on bat, as young children cheer while playing cricket in a not-so-far distance.

Just then, Parveen was handed a mug of tea given by one of the ladies returning from the kiln. Other girls and ladies carried another five or six pots that seemed plenty for the entire group. As the ladies distributed cups, others filled them up and poured out tea.

'Thank you, dear,' she said.

She went on to say, referring to the climate changes, 'It appears like India and Pakistan have been riding on a rollercoaster of extreme weather fluctuations since the late 1970s or as far back as 1968. I cannot remember when our climate was so cruel, intense, and interchangeable.'

Most of the assembly nodded and chatted together without further comments. They patiently watched Parveen's every move and listened with intent, not to miss a single word she spoke.

Parveen went on to say, 'A couple of you—honorable ladies, gentlemen, and not forgetting you, beautiful children—gathered around here now might find it difficult to understand me. As you are aware that I am from Goa which is now a part of India, long time ago, my family moved to Kamoke in the Punjab. Therefore, I have a strange-sounding accent. I know most of you are from around here, the Sindh Province. Basically, what I am trying to say is that now my accent has changed quite a lot since moving down here. Don't want to upset anyone, so therefore, please bear with me as I speak, and if you don't understand my meaning, just shout out. I will get my son to explain everything.'

She glanced around for Mushtaq. She noticed the entire family were not there. She enquired to the group, 'Has anyone seen my family?'

'Oh yes, I did. They went off to gather firewood from the desert,' said one old man.

'Thank you,' Parveen replied.

Parveen asked the group, 'Anyone else here from the Punjab or Goa?'

Everyone glanced around at one another. But nobody answered her back. It looked as if she were the only outsider and no other person were from anywhere else.

'So then if I speak too fast for you to understand my strange accent, you will have to listen a bit quicker,' she said jokingly as the assembly of listeners chuckled.

As she studied the faces of all these poor people, a deep sense of pride crept into her soul. In her mind's eye, she felt as if she were a movie star sitting on one of those TV chat shows and she were the main attraction in the seat.

She settled down to begin her story and was overwhelmed by the amount of intelligent questions coming in from the audience of listeners in the crowd. She also noticed that everyone were either raising their hands or talking over her to have their queries addressed.

Parveen struggled to understand. Anyone in the mille looked totally confused. 'Please, one question at a time. Just raise your hand if you want me to answer your question. I promise to give you a clear answer in good time. Okay then? But please, may it be just one person and one question at a time. Best of all, it would be great if you raise your hand as if I were the school teacher or one of those lecturers in a university campus,' she said with humor.'

Everyone laughed, and Parveen chuckled.

Then such a warm and wonderful feeling came over her. How special she felt, looking around at the smiling faces of her hospitable assembly of listeners.

Soon, Parveen's son Mushtaq arrived, with his wife Asahi and their four children Caleb, Sani, Neela, and Imran.

Mushtaq waved across the heads of the people then said, 'Sorry, Mother. I apologize for us being late. We went to gather up some firewood for our house.' He maneuvered in through the sitting group to find an empty spot to sit on the ground.

'It's okay, Son. I am sure you have not missed any of the story so far. And anyway, you already have heard me tell it so many times before,' replied Parveen. But she felt a little uneasy with their presence.

'Okay, moving forward in my story,' she said, 'it's my honor to be able to extend a warm welcome to each of you latecomers too. Thank you for your interest in me and my family.'

Parveen made a statement, 'As you know, nothing in this life stays the same, but if you are strong enough to accept the changes and forgive the pain that others inflict upon you, only the goodness of God's grace can shine on you in the end.'

With dusk just setting in across the skies, supported by a silky, shimmering red sun casting long shadows that formed an awry picture, with plumes of black smoke bellowing high, the entire skyline was dotted with silhouettes of the night-shift men who could be seen shuffling around here and there on top of the brick kiln as they attended to the task of the process of baking batches of the sun-dried bricks.

Everyone in the assembly had a clear view now of the fire stokers already hard at work. Just another night shift for them began in the Thar Desert's brick kilns and pits.

The kiln dayshift, weary and tired after a long twelve-hour shift, were heading down from the kiln to the waterfall at the base of the overhanging hill—the same location as the pit workers used earlier to wash themselves under the falling water.

COLORFUL BANGLES & BRIGHT COLORED TRADITIONAL
CLOTHING BRIGHTENS UP THE DAY

COLORFUL BANGLES & BRIGHT COLORED TRADITIONAL
CLOTHING BRIGHTENS UP THE DAY

Parveen explained to the gathering as she reminisced on her life as a child. She talked about her couple of years when she lived in Kamoke Town in the Punjab. She stared over their heads as if she could see the scene unfold on a movie screen. She spoke of the many major events that had taken place, leading up to the creation of the Pakistani and Indian nations back on 14 and 15 August 1947.

Parveen commenced by trying to make an excuse for her mindfulness 'You know, it's a very long time ago, and my memory has started to fade a bit on me. It must be almost forty-eight years or more ago. I remember so well when we heard the many rumors that circulated throughout our tightly knit community in the Kamoke railway village.

'Our village is located approximately thirty-four miles or fifty-five kilometres north of Lahore city in the Indian Punjab. The main railway line passes through, carrying passengers from Lahore and Peshawar.

'Kamoke Town comes in under the administration of Gujranwala district counsel of the Punjab. It is said that the village takes its name from the influential Sikh family that resided there. They owned most of the houses, factories, shops, and farmlands in the areas and districts that surround the district. In fact, it stretched out as far as Takakura District to the western side of the town and as far north as Gujranwala.'

Sunday, 20 July 1947

Parveen said, 'One Sunday morning, I decided to go down again to the railway station to help my mother. She left the house earlier that morning to work as a sweeper.

'I had started to cross over the footbridge, just in time to look down at the colorful array of people sitting on the rooftop. Some waved up at me as they flashed past under the bridge. As the smoke from the coal burner dissipated around me and the bridge, I watched it fade away in its distant destination. In those days, most of the trains were always overcrowded. That particular train was heading firstly to Rawalpindi and on to Peshawar. I was a bit upset that I had been late going there to see the passengers and bid them farewell.

'My father—peace be upon him—was employed as the stationmaster before the war. Everyone who ever travelled by rail knew him for his compassion and hospitality. We also felt obliged to carry on his tradition of caring for the people on the trains, especially through Kamoke station. Therefore, they would feel very upset if there was not a member of our family present on the station to show, greet the passengers, and wish the travellers a safe and pleasant trip. My mother would have a couple of bottles of water to give to the children and older women. So early every morning as my mother arrived at the station, her first task was to gather up the empty bottles from the stationmaster's offices. From there, she would head over to the station's shallow well to fill up the bottles with cool water—a task chosen to complete almost each day by my dear mother, especially during the hotter days of summer.

'"But yes, we were too late today," I said to myself. "Never mind, there will be another train arriving soon."

'Everyone in our family knew the schedule of every single train. So I knew that time that the next train will be coming from the northern side and stopping here in Kamoke. Mostly, the trains would only stay for approximately ten minutes before they would have departed to Lahore City.

'It was then I noticed a well-dressed travelling businessman who was reading a copy of the *Delhi Hindustan Weekly Times*. He was sitting alone on a red bench while waiting for this train.

'"Good morning, sir," I said. "Are you going to Lahore today?"

'I stood in front of him with my back towards the station building behind me. I watched the farmers tend their crops behind him in the open fields. I tightened up my shawl, covering my head in front as a sign of respect for the guest.

'"Oh yes, my dear. I am going to Lahore, and maybe this is going to be my last trip in view to what's going on."

'"Oh, sir, please forgive my ignorance," I went on to say as I reached out my hand and introduced myself to the stranger. "Hi, sir. My name is Parveen. I am from this village and live here with my family. My mother works at the station as a sweeper. Can you see her? That's her with the stationmaster over there."

'He replied, "That is a very nice name you have, young lady. By the way, my name is Pradeep Singh. It's my pleasure to meet you today."

'"Oh, you too," I replied.

'Pradeep went on to explain his understanding of the situation. He said, "Do you know that, already, the Muslim league and their supporters from up there are claiming to own this portion of the country?

'"It is my intention to make a hasty escape across the border with my family. They are waiting for me to arrive to Lahore. Hopefully, they should be in the Central station. I already have closed my family tailor-shop business in Peshawar. I had one of the finest properties on the Grand Trunk Road. The shop was facing just across the street from the Peshawar cinema.

'"The angry mob had started to break up some of my friends' homes and businesses. I was not expecting the situation to deteriorate so quick. But very soon, we lost our livelihood and everything we owned. My shop was burned to the ground. Luckily, with just the clothes on our backs, we ran to the train station that is located close to the Mongol Fort. Myself and a couple of my neighbors just kept on running. We were so scared and frightened. Never looked back down the street.

'"As we approached the entrance of the Peshawar Station, there were more men with sticks, waiting to beat anyone not of their creed. We had to fight our way in through the entrance, and with the grace of God, a train was moving slow enough for me to catch hold of, just leaving the station. I was almost out of breath at that particular time. I struggled to jump forwards and managed to hang on to the carriage door. My friends did not make it and were left behind to fend for themselves.

'"So I travelled along on the outside of the train, all the way to Rawalpindi Station. (fourth largest city in Pakistan) There were lots of people on the rooftop. Many of the passengers disembarked there, so from there onwards, I managed to push myself inside to get a seat."

'I listed in silence and could not believe my ears. "Oh, my poor man, can I get you anything?" I asked.

'"They have already started slaughtering Sikhs and Hindi men, women, and children in Northern Punjab and further afield. That is why there are so many people in the last couple of trains that came from the NWFP, the Northwest Frontier Province."

'"That is terrible," I replied.

'The businessman said, "You know, they don't want us here anymore. They will sadly miss our services as they won't do a lot of the municipal jobs our people work at, such as your job, sweeping, and all the other jobs—cleaning public toilets, removal of dead animals from streets, night-soil collections, etc. But our relationship with the Muslims has been great until now.

"Yeah, I know that some of my best co-workers and customers were Muslim. It's not the ordinary working people who want a pure Islamic republic or country. It's because of the politicians and prayer men that the majority of this is taking place. They are pretending it's for a religious reason they want rid of us. But it's our lands, our businesses, our money, or homes they really want."

'I stood with my mouth opened wide. "Truly, sir. I haven't an idea what to say. Only I started to get very concerned about my own family and relations."

'I asked him, "So then, sir, what is happening with the discussions between Gandhi, Nehru, and Jinnah?"

'He reported by saying, "According to what it is written here in this week's newspaper, see the heading of this article, 'The Mighty British Raj Are Leaving India'. The paper is already out of date… so probably, they have made new developments since it was distributed."

'"Have they made progress on our country's divide?" I asked.

'"Oh yes. That too is well under way."

'"Really?" I replied.

'"Yes, it is true." He then pointed to the front page of his newspaper. "Can you read what it says here?" he queried.

'"Yes, sir," I said.

'"The two leaders and the British Raj have come to an agreement. Do you know they have not consulted the people of India, the staff of local governance, or directors and administrators for guidance? Surely, they must understand not many people are going to sit and accept it."

'I said, "But, sir, that's impossible to believe that the British Raj are leaving India. So the partition of India is definitely going ahead. When will this happen, sir?"

'"Hey, have you not noticed that for the last couple of months that it's well under way? And they should be finalized by the middle of this month—August!" he said, frowning and shaking his head. Obviously, he was not in agreement with the decision. I thanked him as he stepped up into a train about to depart to Lahore.

'I wished him a good day and a safe trip to India with his family.

'He looked down from where he was standing in the doorway and said, "I wish you a good life. I'll pray for you. Please take my advice and tell your parents to get the hell out of here before it's too late to go."

'"Okay, sir, and hope you and your family make it through safely to India."

'The last words he said were "Parveen, remember, don't trust anyone. I'm positive you and your family will not be welcomed here when the partition of our fine mother country is over."

'I returned over to the bench, and just as I sat on it, a shout came from the train.

'"Hey there, young lady. Have you ever been to Lahore City?" said a young man. He was standing, leaning out of the train window, looking down on her from above.

'"No," I said in reply.

'He went on to say, "It's a mighty, fabulous place. One could be in Paris, France, while walking around the city. It's absolutely beautiful and bustling with activities to blow your mind away. There are street bars selling Murree beer from a mountain village just north of Rawalpindi City. Beer is available at many of the open-air restaurants set up along the teeming thoroughfares of the Central Lahore District. Most of these venues stay open twenty-four hours every day of the week. I'm sure you would love the fashion, the culture centres, the cinema halls, the theatres, the book libraries, the museums. And there is also a zoo-park on the Mall Road. The zoological gardens are full of exotic wild animals from every corner of the world. There are people from Europe and, of course, good-looking Englishmen like me."

'Listening to him, I felt like jumping up on the train and going on an adventure with him.

'"You could stay with me. I'll buy you a new dress and fancy shoes," he said, half smiling and laughing at the same time through his bright green eyes and highly polished white face and rosy-red cheeks.

'With that, the engineer blew the horn, and the stationary railway guard standing on the platform shouted out, "Now stand back, lady! And you too, children."

'Now the train started gently to roll. I could hear the man call back to me, "Hey there, young lady. I'm staying in Fayette's Hotel on the Mall Road. I'm living in room sixteen. What is your name, young lady?"

'But I was so emotional and embarrassed as I glanced around at the passengers and people on the platform who seemed to be listening intensely to every word of their conversation, so I refused to reply at first. Then I said, "Oh well, why not?" and shouted through both hands clasped around my mouth, "It's Parveen!"

'I hoped he had heard my name over the blasts of the train's whistles. I don't know why I wanted him to know my name, but I said to myself, "I may never know."

'"My name is Parveen. Hey, mister, my name is Parveen."

'Already, he had pulled his head inside the moving train window as the train moved out of the station while sliding the casement window upwards. I do not think he heard me.

I could not hear what he said before that.

'My mother looked on in dismay and seemed to be upset while she leaned up against a red cast bench and listened to every word of the conversation between the young man and her daughter. Then she enquired, "Parveen, who was that young man you were talking to?"

'I replied, "I do not know him, but he is a very handsome man. Did you see his bright green eyes, Mother? And I think he liked me a lot!"

'Mother smiled and said, "Don't you get any fancy ideas now, young lady." Shortly after, she bent down to continue sweeping up rubbish and dust off the platform and placed it into the bin near to the exit.

'"Oh, Parveen, I nearly forgot to shop for dinner. I will be leaving to go to the bazaar now, and if you want to stay here, meet you at the house. Don't spent too much time here. Also, stop talking to handsome strangers, especially when I'm not here to protect you. Please remember that not everyone you happen to meet is innocent and has good intentions. Some people have other things on their minds when they see young ladies out alone, without a male escort to protect them."

'"But, Mother, I am plenty capable of taking care of myself, and moreover, I am only going to stay if the staff are here, and we always look out for each other," I replied. '"Okay, Mother, I will promise to refrain from talking to handsome strangers. And please don't worry. I expect to be going home in about an hour. See you back there."'

'I continued to sweep up the remainder of dirt with Mother's brush. While glancing up, I spotted my mother briskly walking across the overhead footbridge, and she briefly waved down at me standing in the bustling overcrowded platform. When I acknowledged her, she smiled back in my direction and, before long, headed down the steps towards the Grand Trunk Road. There too is a hive of activities, with local transportation waiting to collect the passengers and take them home.

'Porters in immaculate uniforms were blowing whistles and looking sophisticated in their uniforms as they ventured here and there, attending to the needs of the incoming and outgoing passenger trains. Paperboys shouted the headlines from the week-old newspapers from *Hindustan Times* as they maneuvered through the mille of people on the platforms, seeking a sale.

'There was a sight of the bright, flashing eyes of the coolies as they hiked along with a variety of different-sized luggage and baggage. They too are neatly dressed in red turbans with cream salwar kameez uniforms. I observed their feet as they carefully tiptoed past me, managing not to stumble or trip up over my fast-moving brush. I was always amazed as I studied how they maneuvered through the disembarked passengers while carrying neatly stacked items stuck high up on the top of their heads. The array of luggage belonged to the multitude of passengers who had just stepped down earlier from the train. They trailed along behind each coolie, keeping a keen on their belongings as they hastily cascaded down along the platforms to exit out of the station.

'There were many portable street vendor carts selling a variety of spicy foods, drifting along past train windows to offer meals for sale to passengers. Hungry kids peered out from inside the windows, patiently waiting to order a plate of dal or cup of tea. They too had their money held tightly in their grip.

'Time was of the essence. I watched the guard at the rear of the train with a green indicator flag in his hand. He was monitoring the passengers as they embarked and disembarked from the train. He placed the whistle into the front of his mouth, took a deep breath, and with a chest full of air, blew the whistle, at the same time raising the green flag high over his head and swiping it down again in one swift movement. Doors were tightly secured, closed by passengers and porters alike. Services for food take on a faster pace than before. Money and plates are exchanged with the blink of an eye. Before long, the train whistle blew, and it began to move forwards. People waved; children and mothers cried to departing relatives.

'Looking around through the crowds, I noticed my mother standing closely to the railings. As always, she had found someone to chatter with. This time, it was a Muslim cleric from the town. Even though I could not hear the conversation they were engaged in, I could tell it was light-hearted because of the body movements, the smiles, and the short outbursts of laugher. Then as the cleric went on his way, he placed his hand on to his heart and bowed before crossing the road.

'I saluted over to her and shouted, "Hey, Mother! Busy, are we?"

'"Of course, I was only having a joke with the cleric," she replied as she swept the platform with all this movement of people going on. The stationmaster looked down along the platform and signalled to the porter, "It's time for the train to depart."

'The porter blew his whistle and waved his green flag, facing up along the platform towards the train. The train engineer blew the engine horns. The carriage doors were closed. Passengers hastily completed their food orders as the train started gently to roll forwards. Before long, all the commotion was finished, and the station was barely alive.'

Still thinking about the handsome stranger, Parveen reminisced. 'You know, it is funny—that stranger's face is still clear in my memory,' the old lady said. 'I am still amazed as to how I remember all the finery and details and that information today and after all the years too!'

She chuckled and covered her face as Parveen felt a red-flustered grin coming on. 'I have more to tell you as the story goes on where we meet up again.'

Another old lady sitting on the dirt in front of a group of listeners stared up to her face and finally asked her question, 'Do you think you might have made a mistake not going with him?'

The others agreed and waited for her to answer the question.

I hesitated then smiled and said, 'There is plenty more to come in my story. Please wait until I get that far along later before I finish it.

'The handsome young English stranger on the train had also mentioned that many British visitors—international, diplomats, and sometimes even members of the Royal Family—stayed at the prestigious Victorian Fayette's Hotel. The building was constructed by the British way back; it was built in the year of 1880.

'I believed it to be true as that is what the young Englishman told me at the station. He mentioned it during our short but informative conversation.

'The last train had left the station, and the only people who remained there were the food vendor-merchants counting their paper money and coins acquired from selling meals while their children cleaned up their portable food stalls. A couple of young newspaper boys waved the last few papers in front of the stragglers still heading towards the gate, hoping to make a last-minute sale. The porters chatted as they secured the entrance doors to the ticket office, and coolies escorted the last of the remaining passengers off out of the station.

'As I started to walk home from the railway station in the heat of the day, I remembered my mother had stated that morning that this year was one of the driest year in ages and there was a drastic shortage of water in Kamoke, everyone should pray for rains.

'Then I said to myself while thinking that it referred to the conversation at the station with the businessman Pradeep Sikh, "Pradeep's words were very frightening. So much so. I think there is going to be trouble here in our town for us Hindi and Sikhs. We should start to prepare to go to Delhi and stay with our relations there as soon as possible. Hopefully, we can make it safely as the Muslims League supporters, including police and military, are already attacking homes and buildings belonging to our people in other towns and villages. I better talk to mother and try to convince her and the rest of the family it's time to try to escape the violence that, I really believe and fear, is heading our way soon."'

Parveen remembered how she noticed she was getting some evil looks from a gathering of banner-waving men marching along the Grand Trunk Road while passing by a group of Muslim men.

(The GT Road in the Indian subcontinent was developed by the British with many cast iron bridges and surfaced straights along the way. while it was originally constructed by Sher Shah Suri back in the 16th century).

'I decided to run the rest of the way home.'

Parveen said light-heartedly, 'I expected at that stage, the remaining British foreigners must have already had on their PE (physical exercise) training shoes and/or maybe sat up all night, sipping the remainder of their brandy on the edge of their beds.'

While, waiting for the assigned trains to take them far south to *Karachi* Port and tor by road to Port Qasim on the Arabian Sea. From there the British would then go aboard the merchant navy ships that were assigned to take them the rest of the trip home by sea. This was no easy feat as the entire British fleet of both naval and merchant ships were mobilized to fulfil the obligation and complete the operation in one shift move.

'The repatriation of the British from the entire subcontinent would have cost millions of rupees,' said an old man in the group.

'I don't know how much it cost,' replied Parveen. 'But I expect, if you look at the amount of our raw materials and how wealthy they are from ruling our land and peoples and then look around at the amount of poor people barely able to survive, scratch up a meagre living from the earth since then, think to yourself, are we better off without them in our precious country?'

'Did they just go straight home from India?' asked another young boy.

'Maybe they would have to stay months waiting or possibly sent to other colonies around the globe as I don't think England would have room to sustain such a large influx of peoples. As with the war just ending, everyone there were already on rations, and possibilities of getting employment would have been slim,' said Parveen.

'But from what we saw on the platform and heard from some of the gentry, army officers, and infantry soldiers who were waiting on their trains that day in Kamoke, these groups were heading home to England, assembled into sufficient numbers to fill a ship to take them all away to England.'

'Is that country England a very warm and sunny like here, Auntie Parveen?' a little girl asked.

'Oh no, even though England has four seasons—each with three months—called spring, summer, autumn, winter, the entire country that consists of two islands that make up the UK (United Kingdom), with four separate regions, namely, England, Wales, Scotland, and Northern Ireland, all four parts of the UK receive large amounts of rain almost on a daily basis. The skies are a multiple array of shades of grey, and thunderstorms pass through regularly, spreading gales and high winds out across the country. To answer your quest, it's very cold most of the year. I nearly forgot—in winter time, they get very bad snowstorms too,' said Parveen.

'Yeah, kids, I know what you're saying! What's snow? I've only seen it in photographs in a scene of the nativity set in Bethlehem and street scene of Jerusalem.'

'What's nativity?' asked an old Muslim man.

'It's the birth of Jesus, our Christian god.'

'Oh yeah! He's in our Holy Koran. But we only refer to him as one of our prophets, and we call him Isiah, and Miriam his mother.'

'Yes, you are so right,' said Parveen. She went on to say, 'Let's get back on track with my story. Now where was I? Oh yeah, there is one thing for sure,' said Parveen.

'The British prepared themselves for another hasty retreat and disorderly exit and their final retreat from the Indian subcontinent, not unlike the retreat from Kabul to Jalalabad in Afghanistan sometime ago. The Afghan's persevered and were determined never to be ruled by external forces and continue to this very day. A new border came into existence alled the Duran Line, which divides Afghanistan and, back then, former Indian border which is now Pakistan.

'This repulse surely seemed like only yesterday. To many a British soldier still serving in India, possibly their own grandfathers or even fathers would have served in Afghanistan and taken part in those campaigns.'

Parveen sat quietly before proceeding with the story before saying, 'I am an old woman, and every man and his dog remembered those episodes and story told by our grandparents of how the British were brutally beaten in battles and overrun by the Afghans near Jalalabad before they were forced to retreat across the back to Peshawar and Delhi and never returned to Afghanistan since then.'

'My mother,' Parveen said, 'never stopped talking over the years about our grandfather's contribution to the British Raj, which was his life.

'They sent merchants across Goa from surrounding provinces of India. Remember, Goa was still a colony of Portugal. They offered rewards, goods, salary, food, and a career that would take them across the British Empire.

The first task for the big money if they joined up is to go and fight against the Japanese in North Eastern India.'

Parveen said, 'I guess it was his sense of adventure that encouraged him or maybe because all of his friends had signed up to go. My mother could not understand why. Even though he had an imported job that allowed him to travel all over Goa to work in the railway stations, he still decided to leave with his friends from the neighborhood. That day, we watched him hug my grandmother. He was smiling as he left her standing there all alone.'

'But were you not beside her?' said an old lady in the assembly.

'Yes. She ignored. It was impossible to console her. She went into her bedroom and never came out again.

He never looked back at her as she cried and waved at his back as he vanished down the street. Maybe he knows inside he would not be returning home from the war. Only God knows what pain he went through or what went on in his mind that last day as he marched away down the street with the other soldiers. My father was a trainee stationmaster under the guidance of my grandfather.

Soon some older woman from the group came up to Parveen to comfort her.

Parveen said, 'It's okay. I am all right. I can only vaguely remember him when we lived in Goa. I was very young when he went off to war. But I loved to take his old photograph down from Mothers' cabinet where it was kept amongst her special memories. The photograph was enclosed inside a leather frame and glass. How handsome he looked in his uniform even though it was faded to yellow. The effect slowed its age.

'Those other soldiers and his comrades who marched away that same day… some of them were lucky enough to return home to families. They praised my great-grandfather's achievements, and they would mention how bravely he had fought alongside the regiment and all these honorable British gentlemen-soldiers and their magnificent war machines. The stories and information they provided seemed to satisfy my great-grandmother that her husband was a brave soldier, and as she would always say, he was the best stationmaster Goa had ever had.

'It was on Sunday, 10 August,' Parveen said. 'After lunch, there was very little to do in our home. My mother never did household chores on Sunday. She had a superstition about it. Even though she worked six days at the station, she still loved to go down there, watch the trains and people travelling through the town.

I asked my mother, "Do you want to watch the trains today?"

My sister Bulbul and I never had to have asked her twice.

Mother always said, "Perhaps we go there as with nothing better to do today and as you girls also had Sunday off school. She would agree to take us down there.

'"Okay," Mother said, "so get ready, dress up in your finest clothes." We were so happy as we bobbed along, and all three of us walked down though the village. We knew most of the people in our village then and greeted everyone as we passed along the streets to the station platform. We crossed over the footbridge, stopping to lean out over the side to look down at the tracks, then before long, positioned ourselves to sit up on a red cast-iron bench. From there, we could watch the episodes unfold as from this location. We could observe the small railway station building on the far side of the tracks and on both platforms.

'The locals usually commuted by train as regular travellers heading off in either direction. Some folks went south towards Lahore and Karachi, or other people travelled north to Gujranwala, Rawalpindi Cities, or Peshawar City located in the Northwest Frontier Province and the famous Landi Kotal station near the end of the Khyber Pass. From there, commute by road to the Afghan border.

'My mother tightly squeezed my hand. She asked me, "Hey, Parveen, do you notice anything different today?"

'"Yes," I replied. "Everything appeared different than all the other days."

'The stationmaster was rushing about with a clipboard and pen in his hands. A porter watched up the track and peered down at his wristwatch.

'"Bulbul noticed before asking our mother. "Where are the local Indian commuters today and even gathering people on the platforms?"

'"Oh yes," my mother replied. "I forgot what the stationmaster mentioned yesterday. He has been instructed to have the platforms cleared for the British army and other gentlemen to have access to board onto a couple of trains that are to arrive today. I didn't think it was that important, but it looks like it is.

So perhaps that's the reason none of the locals were there that morning. It was because normal timetable was cancelled.

'"The other trains were either delayed or only transporting soldiers?" I asked mother.

'"I would expect so," said my mother.

'Within a few minutes, both platforms were crowded with a multitude of white-faced people in British army military uniforms.

'I asked my mother, "Who are those people, Mother?"

'She replied, "They are British soldiers, and I guess they must be their wives and children. I expect they were gathered up from the many army camps that are scattered all over our country.

'She went on to say, "They are preparing to leave our country and the military cantonments around the Punjab and the city of Lahore. Big changes are about to happen in our lives. It was not that hard to imagine what was going on in their minds."

'I said, "They look sad, Mother. Are they sad?"

'"Yes," said Mother. "Can't you tell by the look of disappointment and by the hollow gaze on their faces?"

'The porter shouted back to the stationmaster, "Sir, here comes the train now!"

'"Okay," he saluted back to the porter as the stationmaster and the British man in uniform directed the gathering of soldiers and civilians alike into small groups. The train finally arrived into the crowded station. The passengers and their belongings are loaded into train carriages as they made hasty arrangements and preparations to leave India and another part of the world in turmoil.'

'Who decided where to draw the lines?' one of her listeners asked.

'Yeah, was it Gandhi and Nehru? Or was it Muhammad Ali Jinnah, 'Quaid-E-Azam' that set out the Radcliffe international boundaries in between Pakistan and India?' asked a young boy.

Parveen said in reply, 'I really don't know, but it's been stated a very important fellow called Mountbatten—they say he is from England—did the job, with one swift movement of a nervously held pencil when using a child's school ruler to draw the lines that divides Pakistan and India. He drew it on a British army survey map.'

'Did you hear that his thumbnail got in the way on passing Kashmir?' Everyone laughed aloud.

Parveen replied, 'Yes, I believe that might be true too!'

But as Parveen spoke, another older man in the group interrupted, and he said, 'Mountbatten did not draw the Radcliffe Line up directly or segregated a total of 450,000 kilometres and its adjoining population of approximately 86 million people.'

He went on to say, 'It was drawn up by a gentleman called Sir Cyril Radcliffe. He was a senior barrister from England, was sent summonsed to India, and set up an office in a hotel.

'According to a newspaper report at the time, it was his task to draw up a contingency plan for the partition process. It was stated he locked himself away in the hotel and never came out of the office. This person was never in India prior to his arrival.

'He based his one selection criteria on statistics gathered over the two hundred years of British occupation. The information provided him with the guidelines that he used to draw the new divide.

'For instance, when an area had to be segregated, he checked how many different ethnic and religious communities lived in the different districts. The ethnic group with the most people, more than likely, were given the land or property. Some entire districts were divided on religious grounds, For example, the state of Kapurthala mostly went to the Muslim community.

'Another major task was to ensure that canals, railway lines, roadways, dams, etc., had not been halved where possible.

So in many places, the new borderlines follow the infrastructures' off-course major rivers, and even mountains could not fall into this category as they ran meandered throughout the entire country of India. A good example of this is, five of the Punjabi rivers run through both sides of the divide.

'Meanwhile, when the barrister was performing this job, many rumors circulated throughout the communities that their villages and homesteads were going to be taken from them and many thousands perished during this period.

'The Sir Cyril Radcliffe finalized the strategic plans and tasks assigned to him and was flown back to England well before the details of the survey maps were handed over to the new rulers of both Indian and Pakistan four days after partition on 17 August.'

Parveen said, 'Anyway, I understand. The nephew of Lord Mountbatten called Prince Phillip Mountbatten was engaged to Princess Elizabeth in July 1947. They later went on to marry in Westminster Abbey. Princess Elizabeth became Queen of England and the British Empire.'

An old man in the assembly stated, 'You know that Princess Elizabeth had a place of high a steam in the hearts of the Indian people.'

'Yes,' replied Parveen and sanctioned by the other listeners in the group.

'Anyway,' said Parveen, 'the Radcliffe pencil line continued to meander down the map and divided the Punjab into two parts, with one half cutting the portion that is now called Pakistan and the other half portion called India.

'The Thar Desert somehow avoided being split but, with the influx of well over 1.3 million people, caused another vibrant ancient community to be devastated. This set the communities and food chain back up to forty or fifty years.

'Thank you, Uncle, for that information,' she said. 'I was not aware of some of the stuff talked about. I will do my best to remember that for future references and chats like the one we are having tonight.'

The old man humbly bowed and touched both of Parveen's feet in a gesture of respect—a common practice and custom in their tradition.

'Okay,' Parveen continued. 'The urgency of the draw-up of the Radcliffe Line was mainly because it seemed like a sensible solution by the British rulers of India who were in hast to depart from the region.

'I don't think they had an idea about the devastating effect on local cultures, traditional boundaries, and the country this would have.' The old lady sighed. 'But to be certain, they knew the ships were waiting in the harbor as their thoughts of an honorable retreat with dignity failed and the coexistence of a one Indian nation crumbled around them.'

Parveen squinted as she looked up at the Pakistani national flag silently fluttering in the moonlit night. As the flag struggled to move in the light evening breeze, she said to the group of listeners, 'I'm still not sure if the ex-ruling British came from an island faraway from our land, where it's stated their empire has a flag called *the Union Jack*. People around here used to say 'The sun never sets on their flag' as the British Empire is spread out across the globe.'

She went on to say, 'If they believed the "divide and conquer tactic" would work in our sacred land as the order of the day, it didn't. Just look around you and see the mayhem and the disasters they left behind them. Our neighbors are our enemies. Our sons and daughters live in the shadows. Our land is in ruins. Most of all, our souls will never rest in peace. I believe the people who formed this divide through our motherland really have a lot to answer for.

'I understand Mountbatten was a good man and he was just following his country's orders. The master plan to finalize the occupation of the Indian subcontinent, a lot of people say, was because the Second World War left the British in bankruptcy. The empire started to crumble around them. This led to the creation of the British Commonwealth. Queen Elizabeth has been queen of the UK, Canada, Australia, and New Zealand since February 1952. Also, she is still administering her powers to countries—to name a few, Antigua, Belize, Barbuda, Barbados, Grenada, Papua New Guinea, Solomon Islands, Saint Lucia, Saint Kitts and Nevis, Saint Vincent and the Grenadines, and a few more.

'The monarchy managed to maintain a foothold on the purse strings of its former colonies and loyal subjects around the world even though we were mainly a Hindu family with traces of a couple of other religions there too!

'Our family, originally, are from Goa on the western coast of India—a former Portuguese colony—and remained so until the late '70s partitioned our country. Goa is where my grandparents and ancestors derive from. At home, the family communicated in English and Portuguese. Dad loved to take us kids fishing down along the shimmering, sandy white beaches. On other occasions, he would take us in his boat. Our house was situated close to the ocean. Fishermen would come over to our home, and Dad would bring out his home-brew beers, and they would sing sea-shanty songs into the small hours of the morning. Happily, us kids listened until we faded off into our dreams.

'Dad owned a small boat and shared it with our extended family and friends. This is where we spent many a weekend cruising the waters and down the local coast to pass the time away up.

'Sometimes if Dad could not catch a fish, my father would buy a fresh one or two from the fishermen. Then when we arrived back home, my dad would pretend to our mother that he managed to catch them. At the time, she knew quite well he was not much of a fisherman as she had experienced this when they were courting before they got married. She used to say he was afraid to hold a living fish in his hand. But to amuse him, she would definitely go along with his story, pretending to believe him. We watched on in amazement as the joke unfolded. Yeah, it was a laugh back then.' Parveen chuckled in good humor and pride for her family.

'Why did your family move from Goa to Kamoke Town?' one of the group asked Parveen.

'My father worked for the Goa National Railway. That network was run by the Portuguese expatriate workforce.

He was employed by them in the capacity as stationmaster serving in several stations around Goa, and his superiors were instructed by the higher-ups to relocate him far away from our home town. He wasn't happy to be away so far from his wife and us children. So it's just by faith alone we ended up in Kamoke Town. As he got the position, our family had to go too as we had to vacate the house in Goa.

'This was before he went to work throughout the provinces of India and the national Indian railway.

But it was good for us. That was before he got drafted to join up in the Indian army and a sent off to war.

Mom and the family were always dreaded fetching the mail from the local Kamoke post office down in the village, reasons being in case there was bad news from the government war officials about my dad. We never stopped praying for his safe return.

But sadly, it happened the Indian army sent a very insensitive blunt couple of lines in a letter which stated, "Dearest Mrs De Souza, the honorable commanders of the Indian army hereby inform you that your husband Sanjay Sandeep was killed in action, and we regret your loss.'"

Parveen said, 'His comrades of every caste and creed gathered up his remains and in the tradition of his religious beliefs. They held a cremation ceremony in accordance to his last wishes. It was to take place close to where he fought on the banks of the Chindwin River in the vicinity of the battlefield.'

A learnt old man continued to explain the event as Parveen took a toilet break, 'The conflict commenced when Japanese forces were sent to Burma. The British retreated from Burma in 1942, allowing the Japanese army access to their country that brought them right into the Eastern Indian state.

'Lieutenant General Mataucha (Japanese), in order to prevent a British counteroffensive back into Burma, ordered his forces to proceed on an offensive after the British forces into Imphal and Kohima in the state of Manipur, Northeast India.

'The main objective was to try and proceed deep into the interior of India. Rumors at the time were the Japanese were in contact with Mahatma Gandhi and offered their assistance to help push the British Raj out of the Indian subcontinent. The country was already being convulsed by a home-grown independence movement with effectiveness. Mataucha had encouraged support from Indian soldiers who surrendered during the fall of Malaya and Singapore.

'With all signs that the Japanese were organizing an attack, the British requested the assistance of the Americans to provide air support. A tactical manoeuvre was performed by the British who withdrew the ground forces from Burma and prepared a ring of defensive positions in the high ground around the Imphal Valley. This ploy was applied with the intention of encouraging the Japanese forces to be drawn away from their sources and isolate them from their stream of support and supplies.

'It was stated that the British high command believed that the Japanese would not easily cross the nearly impenetrable jungles around Kohima in force. They were very surprized when a full division of approximately fifteen thousand Japanese foot soldiers attacked from the undergrowth and almost wiped out the entire group.

'The last letter my mother received from my father came after he was killed in the battle. He mentioned that they couldn't defend the perimeter of the town. "Every day and night, our men are shot by snipers shooting from inside the dense jungles that surrounded most of the area," he said too. "I don't think we are going to win this fight. The Japanese are good fighters. They do not seem to care if they live or die as we (Indian soldiers) struggle to defend our position. We, likewise, are killing hundreds of them. But the wave of soldiers continues to attack us. The district we are protecting is beautiful with plenty of wildlife. Our defense consists of a contingent of around twelve hundred British and Indian soldiers. We are working together in one location with a combined and consolidated fighting force."

'The defense plot failed as the Japanese made good their advances. They managed to encircle the entire British and Indian positions. The Japanese forces were effective and forced them to retreat, perhaps because of a backfire, meaning supplies, food, and water were finished. Those who survived were either shell-shocked or injured as they returned on a goods train to hospitals around Delhi. Another battle forgotten in history. Those who died have no memorial ceremonies and are forgotten warriors of our country. But not my father. I still light a candle for him and his fellow dead soldier friends.'

One Day in 3 July 1944, Japanese Retreat

'The Japanese and the Allied forces battled long and hard to hold on to the ground they had gained but eventually ran out of rations, ammunitions, and were overwhelmed by the British, Indian with American air support that ended the encirclement around them. And the siege collapsed around Kohima and Imphal. We believed my father was one of the last soldiers to be killed on that day.

Parveen returned and thank the old learnt man for his contribution.

'Parveen, excuse me but did your mother get money when your dad was off fighting in the Second World War?' one small boy asked the old lady.

'The average salaries were a mere twenty-five rupees for one month,' stated Parveen. 'That was considered a good income back in 1943 up to '47, and with Mother's income of five or six rupees per month sweeping the station, we were quite well heeled and well fed. We were better off than most families and farm laborers living within our community. Many of them got paid in a bartering type of way. They were not given money as a reward for their services rendered. Instead, they would receive bags of flour, wheat, chickens, or a bunch of sugar-cane stalks. My mother honored the simplicity of Gandhi's way of life and shared foods or even money. She would give to the poor within the community.'

'Our family,' Parveen said, 'had a comfortable railway housing near the station, consisting of three bedrooms. Bulbul and I slept in one, my brother in another, and parents in the master bedroom. There was a front and back garden and a wide veranda.

'Unfortunately, we had to move out when Dad didn't come back from the war. My mother worked on the sweepers team at the Kamoke local station under the control of the new stationmaster who replaced her husband in his position. She was one of four other sweepers. They would clean the carriages before passengers arrived and changed out of the other train before it was scheduled to depart.

'I can tell you, we were comfortably living in Punjab back then. As far as we were aware, all religions and ethnic communities seemed to get on well together. We as kids played sports with everyone. We really had a happy lifestyle. Even though we were poor, we were happy. I remember,' she said, 'our Muslim property owner early in the morning came knocking at our front door. It was 7 August.

'It seemed like everyone in the town were talking about the major event about to take place on 14 August, with the creation of the New Dominion of Pakistan (later named the Islamic Republic of Pakistan) coming into reality, with Muhammad Ali Jinnah (Quaid-E-Azam) sworn in. He became the country's first governor general in the new nation's capital called Karachi.

'Back then, on that very Thursday, our landlord came to our rented house and introduced his younger brother, his wife, and family. They had just arrived after travelling through all the mayhem from Bangalore. They looked very tired. I could tell by the way they moved through our house that they had other intentions. There was a lot of whispering going on between the two brothers. Therefore, I could tell by the look on his face that he had very little options but to ask us to leave our rented home as his brother and family intended to move in. The shock was devastating to our entire family.

'The landlords gave us three hours to pack up our belongings. We had no transport to carry the furniture, so my mother requested him for permission to store it in his garden sheds. She intended to send some of our relatives to collect it whenever we reached their home over the border in India.

'Another knock came on the door after two hours. It was the landlord with his brother again. He began to push my mother and demanded more money. As she opened her bag to give him some money, the brother grabbed it from her and emptied it onto the floor. He helped himself to all the money she was saving for a rainy day. "Oh please, mister," she pleaded with him to have mercy on her. With this, he started to beat her around the head. My little brother tried to protect her. But he too was beaten. Before long, we were evicted and placed out on to the street, with nothing more than the clothes on our backs and nowhere to go.

'Quietly, we stood there. I remember that sad face of my mother as she held on tightly to us children. There wasn't a friendly face on the streets, and they were full of thieves, murderers, and people running in every direction. As we hastily ran as a family in a group of four heading down towards the railway, Mother said some of her friends down there at the station would help us, and hopefully, she could convince one of them to loan us enough money to use as train fare to Firozpur or Amritsar.

'Mother said, "We have relatives who live there too." I remember she always talked about our uncle and how brilliant a Taylor he was, how he had learnt his trade in the army apprentice school in Bombay. He has his own very successful clientele of rich Sikh businessmen who brought all his men three-piece suits and shipped them to their high-street shops in Downtown London.

'As we discussed our uncle, my mother stopped short and started staring down the road. She had spotted a man from our street. He was running in the opposite direction from where he lived. The poor man had blood gushing from his side onto his white shirt from his right-hand side. Even though he was clearly in great pain, his concern for our safety was unbelievable.

'My mother asked him, "What has happened to you? Can I help you, mister?"

'"No, don't worry about me, please," he said in a humble sort of way. "They…," he said as he pointed down the road through the madness, "Those men… They have just killed my wife and son. We didn't do anything to deserve such an assault. We had just come from shopping in the markets and bazaar in town down there on the corner, and now they are coming to kill me. But I managed to break free. I suggest you need to run quick run. There they are over there. Please, misses, try to run as fast as you can. Come this way!" With this, they spotted us looking in their direction as the heavily armed group of men started to run, heading our way after us.

'We all started to run along with him. Through the mille of people, we could see the mobs were looting many houses. Some buildings were burning. We could see the dead and injured people. Dying animals were to be seen everywhere we looked. The roads were covered in red blood, and we found it hard to remain upright as we slipped and climbed over the dead and dying as we went. It was hard to see or find friends, family, or familiar faces as we rushed through the crowds. Everything was happening as I looked around and noticed my mother and brother was not there beside us anymore and had disappeared.

'"Oh no," I said, holding on tightly to my younger sister Bulbul's hand. We both cried out through the rush of people. "Mommy, Brother, where are you?" But we never managed to find them.

'This was the last time we ever saw my mother and brother again. We hid in a culvert under the track lines and waited there. We hoped it all might end soon so then we could go look for our mom and brother.

'My sister said, "Don't cry, Parveen. We will find them soon. Maybe they made it to the station and are waiting on us catching up on them."

'"Yes, hopefully, you are right," said I.

'"But it's not safe to leave here this smelly, dirty culvert yet."

'The smell came from outside the culvert as it was commonly used by everyone as a toilet, and the smell was unbearable. But we had no choice only to stay put.'

A listener in the group called out and said, "Parveen, what did you and Bulbul, your sister, do next?"

A depressed feeling came over her as she proceeded by saying, 'A few men walked up to the outside of the culvert and started to urinate, facing in our direction. Luckily, it was dark enough, so they could not see us hiding in the small culvert. But my sister and I were shocked at what we saw, and they relieved themselves. I pulled Bulbul by the arm, and we quickly left out the far side of the culvert. We were so scared, we didn't dare turn around. And I warned my sister not to look back and climb up the embankment and over the gravel siding of the steel railway lines. From there, we ran back across the railway tracks now facing the Grand Trunk Road and the town of Kamoke beyond that.

'This time, we looked over to the right and could see an overcrowded passenger train coming from the north direction. Many people—young and old—were running across the railway lines heading in both sides to cross the tracks. There was a variety of different groups of people—Hindus, Sikhs, Christians, and Muslims—everyone trying to safeguard their family members. I can still hear… the cries are still fresh in my mind.

'I noticed an elderly man bend over from old age, struggling to walk with the aid of walking stick. As he hesitantly maneuvered through the crowd, he started tripping over and fell right in front of the black steam-driven engine train. I don't believe that the engineer even noticed the old man. But to line up and stop directly in front of the platform on the station, he had started to apply the brakes.

'The train's wheels gave off a high-powered screech as it puffed on towards the station platform. The combination of water, steam, and fire ushered it forward. I turned away. I didn't want to watch the poor old man die. But nobody tried to help him before the man was run over and cut into pieces by the train. I managed to pull myself and sister Bulbul across in time—or we too nearly met with the same faith as he did—but managed to scrape through a group of women and children heading in the same direction as us.

'I think there were a few other people killed or injured as the train travelled along the short distance into our town Kamoke.

'The engineer shunted the engine and tooted on the whistle with black soot bellowing out of the chimney as it slowed down and came to a sudden jerky stop in front of the station. As bystanders looked on. The entire platforms vibrated beneath their feet. There were people standing on the rooftops of the carriages, while others leaned or hung out of the windows and open doors. Some of them jumped off to run to go to relieve themselves, only to be attacked by the waiting local crowd.

'The police managed to persuade the raged crowd away from the train and platform to the outside of the station. The sun had already gone down by now. It was early evening. I would say around eight o'clock.'

Parveen glanced around at the circle of bright-eyed men and women who were listening intensely to every word. She continued to tell her story, 'The frightened passengers had not received any provisions since they left on their journey. It was expected that the train was destined to go straight to Firozpur. Kids on the train were asking their parents, "What's happening? Why are we stopped here?"

'"What's this place called, Daddy?" a little girl asked.

'"I don't know," he replied.

'"Why have they not given us any food or water, Daddy?"

'A wise old Hindu bearded man replied, "It's because we are Hindus and Sikhs. These people they believe we are untouchables."

'"So they believe we are not good enough to eat their food or drink their water," said the little girl.

'That's right' he replied.

'The majority of the passengers sat, observed everything that was going on that night in the dark carriages. At the break of dawn, a large contingent of police and army arrived in a convoy of trucks from the direction of Lahore. They struggled to get pass through the large crowd that accumulated outside the station overnight. There were Muslim men and boys in their hundreds, chanting death to the non-Muslim infidels. The police officers did nothing to encourage the engineer to get the train moving on its journey.

But instead, they added to the problem by commencing a body search of the occupants and their belongings inside the train. No one was spared in the search. Women and young girls were made to strip almost naked in front of their families and the other passengers before they too were being manhandled and abused by soldiers and some of the police constabulary.

'Considering this, some Hindu and Sikh fathers could not bear it to happen and started to take the lives of their wives and daughters. I would say, it's a maybe because they'd rather have them die at their own hands than let them be raped or murdered at the hands of these hooligans.

'The police constabulary search had recovered a variety of old Lee–Enfield rifles, small 9 mm pistols, and other types of arms and weapons. It was a one-sided pitch fight in the making. As soon as they stepped out of the train, they distributed them to the local crowd. Shortly after, there was a strange silence that ascended over the station platform—a lull before the storm, so to speak. During the brief calm, it seemed like the entire train was loaded to the hilt, with people about to be given the opportunity to leave the station.

'The engineer of the train was hastily preparing to depart—a humble beginning, a sign of compassion—as the steam-engine train panted while the whistle echoed out through the tiny town. Little did anyone know what was planned to happen next.

'People stared out of the train towards the uniformed authorities as they covered their ears to the muffled high-pitched sound filling the air. This enticed the heavily armed crowd to charge into the station again for the second time, and they freely attacked the passengers by firing off volleys of rifles, and small arm revolvers shot into the skies. Others were beating the unarmed and innocent bystanders or whomever they came across and who looked Hindu or Sikh with axes, hammers, swords, and knives. Most of the violence was initially directed at the Sikh and Hindi menfolk on the train, followed on by beating all who resisted their demands or disobeyed their animalistic demands to hand over personal possessions.

'The maddening crowd managed to enter some of the compartments. The Hindi and Sikh really had no chance to survive as they had been disarmed shortly before. Giving the mob the upper hand, they met with little resistance as they killed all in their path—men, women and children.

The crowd looted anything they could get their hands on. It was not long after the senior police officers and their men joined in by firing into the train. Moreover, many were not lucky enough to be able to get escape. They were shot dead by either the police or the crowd. Many of the injured passengers inside the train, along with their family members, were systematically butchered. Most were helpless as they lay huddled together in their seats.

'During a lull in the carnage, some opportunist Muslim men grabbed women and young kids and dragged them away for their own pleasure. We were so scared that we might get shot, raped, or stabbed without warning. Suddenly, we were confronted by a man who grabbed both of us around the shoulders. I remember screaming and struggling to break free from his powerful grip. He was saying, "Stop it now, Parveen. I'm going to help get you and your sister Bulbul to safety." As I looked up, I noticed he was the grey-haired stationmaster. "It's okay," he said. "Now come quickly," he said as he walked us in through the main station building. We passed police, porters, orderlies, and some injured soldiers.

'We were bundled into the small ticket office as he proceeded to fetch his bag from his office. On his return, he enquired, "Where are your mother and younger brother?"

'I tried to tell him what had happened up our street, but he interrupted me and said, "Okay, we should move quickly if we are going to survive."

'"Where are you taking us?" I asked him.

'"The train engineering team are unhitching the steam-engine and coal trolley from the first carriage. We are going with them to Lahore Central railway station."

'"Please, sir. Please find my mom and little brother."

'"I'm sorry," he replied. "I've looked everywhere, and there's no time left."

'A couple of soldiers shielded us in between them as they nervously ushered us forwards before pushing us up and into the engine cabin. Steam and smoke were streaming out from almost every direction of this beastlike mechanism. The crew was heavily sweating, with soot-covered faces. They were busily shovelling coal into a bucket and manhandling it forward and then emptying it upside down inside the red-hot furnace. As they slammed the small cast-iron door closed, I watched in amazement how the engineer was twisting knobs checking gauges, and pushing levers as he rushed from side to side, checking for the signalman to change the lever to the "go" status. He glanced down as we sat on the floor as he hurriedly prepared the mighty beastlike engine for departure. I smiled across at Bulbul who was squashed up tight beside me on the floor.

KAMOKE STATION PUNJAB 1947 (IMAGE)

'We both watched in astonishment at the performance of these two highly skilled technicians with sweat dripping down their faces from the heat of the furnace. With the preps ready, with a jerky shutter, the engine puff and pulled the train along. After a while, when the train was up to speed and away from the village, the engineer invited us to stand at the small door. It was a scary feeling as trees and fields flashed past. The movement of wind and smoke scraped our long hair away from our faces. Strange warmed from the hot furnace behind our backs. We were amazed to notice some soldiers were clinging on to the side panel as they sat along the trolley over the wheels of the engine.

'The stationmaster spotted us looking down and informed us that the soldiers were there for our protection. He stated they were guarding the train against attacks from bandits and mobs. "Don't look so worried," he said. "They are professional soldiers and will kill anyone who tries to stop the train and will escort us all the way to our destination, the Lahore City station."

'With the news, we girls seemed to settle back and felt safe as never ever before on the journey. Fantastic experience. We never had anything like this trip to Lahore City before. I felt sad, *if only mom and my brother were here to experience it.*

'Before long, we were well on our way out to the open countryside. As the train, for a part, ran parallel to the Grand Trunk Road, we noticed that streams of people were on the move too. There were hundreds of them, even thousands—a sign that the old businessman I met in the station was right. Looking back towards Kamoke village, I said to Bulbul, "Where can Mother and Brother have gone?"

'We pondered awhile as the flat, unattended green fields rolled out across the horizon. The trip seemed endless, and now we're feeling tired, and we spoke as to what Lahore City was going to be like. I told my sister Bulbul of the wonderful places we were going to be able to visit, just as I was told by the handsome stranger on the train in Kamoke railway station.

On our approach to the central station, we passed over the Ravi River. It was so big and majestic in all its splendor. Children were playing and swimming with their domestic water buffaloes along the banks of the river. Next, we travelled across hundreds of railway tracks heading in every direction possible before reaching the biggest station in all the Punjab but passed right though it and into a siding and sauntering yard full of many other steam engines and guarded by hundreds of armed soldiers and security personnel.

'"What are they doing with all the trains?" asked Bulbul.

'"We have been directed to take them to Lahore to save them from being confiscated by the pro-Indian individuals wanting to take every engine, carriages, and railway equipment over to the Indian side to be under the control of the Delhi municipality," said the engineer. "So whenever the troubles are finalized and the partition is completed, the new nation will have their own public transport in Pakistan."

'"But, sir," said Bulbul, "didn't you say you were going to cross over and live on the Indian side of the border soon?"

'"Yes, that is true, but for now, I have fulfilled my directors' instructions and delivered this engine to Lahore Central station."

'The two of us girls stood in the huge depot on an oil- and grease-covered work platform, waiting on the two men to take us to the city. We watched as more and more trains arrived from different parts of the country. It was amazing to see so many workmen moving around tools and equipment and servicing the steam engines, all in a clock-like manner.

'The time passed without notice. Maybe we were there for one or two hours. But it was four hours. The men finalized extinguishing the fire in the furnace. The stationmaster said, "It's his duty to make sure the fire is totally doused for safety reasons. Just imagine if he ignored the safety rules and a spark fell onto the grease and oil. It would ignite a fire and burn down the entire station."

'The engineer shouted over to us girls standing with the stationmaster, "We are finished now. Just let me go wash my hands and face, and we can go." He wandered off to the men's toilets as he went to drink from a drinking water fountain, smiled back in our direction, and beckoned us to come take a drink too. We approached the fountain and enjoyed a drink of cool, refreshing water. Before long, the engineer joined us, and we stood there for a while. He seemed sad as he glanced back at his train engine. I swore I saw a tear in the side of his eye. After all, he had worked all on this steam engine since he was a boy. I believe the stationmaster noticed his teary eyes and sadness. I think, in order not to embarrass him any further, he said, "Now what are we going to do with you two girls?"

'The engineer replied, "If it's okay with you, sir, and if the young girls agree, I'll take them to my house as my wife and I would enjoy the company as we don't have any children. She is getting old and sure could do with some help around our house. They would be safeguarded, well fed, and happy until we can find their mother and the rest of their family members.

'"Oh no. We want to go to my relatives in Fayette's Hotel on Mall Road," I said, crossing her fingers behind her back. Bulbul looked across at her, amazed with hearing the information for the first time in her life.

'"Do we really have living relatives in Lahore City? I never heard Mother talk about them," said Bulbul.

'"Shush, girl. Yes, it's true," I replied. You never heard or met them because Mother was not talking to them over some issues a long time ago. Therefore, that's the reason you never heard about them yet."

'On hearing this, both men looked at each other and agreed to let us go to the hotel. "Okay then," said the engineer. "I will take you all the way there. It's out of my way, but it is still early, and I will take a Tonga (horse and cart) back to my house most of the way there as I live down that way. So I will drop you off at the hotel on Mall Road. He went on to state, "You know, this road runs right through the city, and it is a very long road. So we will need to eat something. Here, take this food and water." Earlier that morning, he had prepared some bread, vegetables, and bottled water to eat along the way to Lahore.

'"Oh, thank you very much, sir!" Parveen said to him. "And thank you both for everything."

The engineer acted like a tourist guide pointing out the different British buildings such as the GPO, the central courts, the museum as well as Regal Chowk (the name of the crossroads) at Temple Road, and a Christian cathedral—all the places her handsome stranger on the train had mentioned back in Kamoke. Yes, he was right… only thing he didn't mention was the traffic and all the people.

'The city was a hive of activity with all types of people, many with all their worldly possessions in tow. Some have rickety old carts, and others have trucks and buses. Everyone seemed to be traveling in different directions. The girls paused briefly to watch as the engineer went down a side road heading home. The sun was high in the afternoon sky and extremely hot.

'"Bulbul, are you hungry now?"

'"Yes, Parveen! I'm starving," she replied.

'"Okay let's sit over there in between the two roads. Nice shade and beautiful green grass too." As we ate the food and drank the water directly out of the bottle, we watched almost every form of transport carrying masses of extended families passing before us.

'Bulbul said, "Too many people, and why are they looking so sad? I expect they are in the same situation as we are in—losing their home and love ones and facing an uncertain future or destiny."

'"Yes," I said. "It is time we get moving. I do not like the way some of these men are looking at us."

'We clumsily staggered to our feet, leaving the remains of our meal to the crows who were eagerly waiting a chance to devour it. We watched as they flew down and scavenged everything in their path.

'I outstretched my hand to take Bulbul's hand to make sure we stayed together as we proceeded towards Fayette's Hotel.

'It was a beautiful day as we strolled along through the busy rush of people along the footpaths. We walked past the railings surrounding the zoo park as we went along. Bulbul, my sister, enquired as to who are our relatives were in Fayette's Hotel. I was afraid to tell her that I had told a lie to the good stationmaster back there but began to explain to her about the nicest foreigner I had ever laid eyes upon. "We're going to be very happy in his company. He'll buy us fancy shoes and nice-fashioned clothes to wear."

'Bulbul said, "I hope he's not a rapist or a murderer or slave trader or—"

'"Oh, stop it," I said to Bulbul. "He is a very nice man."

'"What does he work then?" my sister asked.

'"I do not know, but he looks like he is from high society, or maybe he is a doctor or somebody important. I really do not know."

'"We walked in silence along the remainder of this road and, as we approached the hotel gates, looked down the busy driveway that led up to the canopy surrounding the main entrance doors. As we stood outside on the road, under the shade of one of the many large leafy trees that lined up along both sides of the road, Bulbul said, "Well then, are we going in or not?"

'"Okay," I replied, "let's do it."

'*What if he is not here anymore?* I thought. *What will we do then? Where would we go? I should have got the engineer's address.* "Okay," I said. "Please, oh please be there, Mr Tom. Please be living in room number sixteen."

'I felt sick inside as we approached the revolving entrance doors. We stood back, waiting on a chance to jump in one of the glass-panelled doors. A porter called out, "Ladies, please, this way," pointing to a side door already open.

'"Thank you, mister," I said.

'"Before long, we walk in to the high-ceiled lobby, and before long, we're confronted by another porter. Good afternoon, young ladies. And how can I help you?" he said.

'"We are looking for my sister's friend," replied my little sister.

'I too said, "Yes, sir. He is residing in room number sixteen. Can you please tell him we are here from Kamoke railway station, just north of Lahore City? Please inform him that Parveen and my sister Bulbul are here to meet him. Oh, also mention it is very urgent and important we see him today as we have nowhere else to go because of the events that are happening all over the country. We are very desperate and honorable young ladies of good repute."

'"Okay, I believe he is in the hotel. Please take a seat over there." He pointed to a large leather seat. "You can sit over there. I'll go and find him for you. It will only take me a moment."

'The porter hurriedly vanished off in the direction of a long hallway with doorways dotted down along each side. I pictured Mr Tom framed into the train-carriage window way back then. *I hope he remembers me*, I thought. We went to find him, and before long, my handsome stranger was standing in front of me.

'"Well, hello," he said. "And you remember me and my room number! Clever little lass you are."

'I blushed and shyly lowered my eyes to the floor.

'"What is that black stuff on your clothes and faces?" Mr Tom enquired.

'"It's coal soot and fumes of smoke that came from the steam-engine train and general dirt from the long journey here from Kamoke Village," I reported.

'Mr Tom looked around at the faces of the regular residents and their guests, many of whom were heading into the bar for evening pre-dinner drinks. *Is it that time already?* he thought as he pulled his pocket watch out as if to reassure his curiosity. "Oh then," he said, "what am I going to do with you, young ladies?" He looked concerned and flustered, and while he greeted some people passing by, for a short while, he fidgeted around the lobby before saying, "Okay, let's get you ladies a room. I will introduce you to Marilyn. Wait here. I will go get her from our room. Surely, she can find you a change of clothes from her closet."

'While waiting on Mr Tom's lady Marilyn to arrive in the lobby, I overheard a conversation between an Anglo-Indian lady and some staffers at the reception desk. I got up from where Bulbul and I were sitting and approached the counter and politely enquired from the older lady, "Oh, madam, please forgive me for interrupting you, but I would like to ask you, are you from Goa?" I stood at the outer side of the counter in a very humble and respectful way.

'The old lady stopped talking and, for a moment, stood motionless and replied, "Why yes, I am. How did you identify that? Was it my accent or the way I am dressed?" she responded.

'I stated, "I identified your accent from that of my parents. We are originally from Goa too. My father worked on the Portuguese railway as a stationmaster, and we had to move to Punjab because he got a job at the Kamoke railway station."

'"Oh, my poor darling children," she replied. "What has happened to you? Look at you two girls! You are full of soot and smell of train smoke. Where are your father and mother? Are you girls staying as residents in our hotel?"

'"We hope to stay as guests of Mr Tom. We are very tired after escaping the terrible disaster across the countryside."

'Bulbul then approached the counter and started to cry, "I miss my mother and brother. We don't know where they are."

'"Settle down. Let's go find Mr Tom."

'"Oh yes, ma'am," I said. "We have lost our dear mother and our younger brother back there in Kamoke Town, and our dear father—Lord, have mercy on his soul—was killed while he was serving in the national army of India at war for our homeland, India."

'"Hmmm, that is a very sad state of affairs. As Mrs Braganza stated, nobody seemed to remember then, especially with the turmoil and happenings here and now."

'"Yes, madam. You are right," I said in response.

'As we walked along the corridor towards Mr Tom's room, I explained to Mrs Braganza how I had met Mr Tom in Kamoke railway station, how he invited me to come down to Lahore City. "I never believed I would need to come here ever. But given the situation Bulbul and I are now in, he has promised he's going to help us settle until we can find our family again. Please, we hope that we are not any bother and can help around the hotel."

'"Oh yes," said Bulbul. "We can wash dishes and bedding if you need help."

'"Oh no, come on, young ladies. Thank you for your offer, but there are plenty of staff to attend to that. I just want you to feel at home here in the hotel.

Okay, make yourselves at home, and if you need me, just ask the staff to get me. My name is Mama Braganza, but you can call me Mavis. That's my favorite name! My husband's name is Eddy. Our family own this hotel, at least for the moment. There are rumors going about that when this part of India becomes Pakistan, the new government will nationalize all the privately-owned hotels and the Christian schools and hospitals. I am worried about that," she said.

'With this, Mr Tom's bedroom door opened. "There you are." He returned with a young English lady. He introduced us to Marilyn, his fiancé and went on to say, "Marilyn and I are engaged to be married next year."

'"Oh, that's very nice," I said begrudgingly and in a funny way relieved and happy to hear he was not a rapist. I smiled across, and Bulbul too seemed to approve of the arrangement.

'"Thank you, Mavis. We will look after Bulbul and Parveen from here. This is your room," he said, pointing to room number seventeen.

'"Okay, Marilyn's going to take you girls and make you into princesses before dinner," said Mr Tom as he glanced down the collider towards a group of residents heading into the bar.

'I said, "I will catch up with you for dinner then."

'"See you in about an hour or so," Marilyn said. He waved back as he briskly walked away in the direction of the bar.

'Marilyn, Bulbul, and I strolled across through the well-manicured gardens. We studied the beauty and splendor of the finest Victorian architecture and verandas. At that moment, I believed my sister Bulbul and I must have died and just entered paradise.

'When we walked into our room, we stood just inside the door, glancing around at the lavishly decorated high ceilings and two slow-moving fans with cool air. The external wall facing the gardens had two longitudinal sliding casement windows. The windows were draped out with white-laced curtains and long navy-blue ceiling-to-floor curtains. We walked over to look out onto a lush green lawn. Surrounded by rose trees and in the centre stood one tall mango tree. "Oh, look over there. Is that a swing ride swaying in the breeze?"

'How happy and excited we were. Marilyn washed us in a pearly white bath filled to the brim with bubbles and silky, smooth, hot water. She was humming a song, "London Town is falling down, falling down, falling down." She told us stories about London Town and the Big Ben Tower and Clock and how she missed her family and girlfriends. Marilyn's eyes danced in her head as she reminisced about ballroom dancing and the other boys she dated before meeting Mr Tom.

'I enjoyed her stories as we listened with keen interest and visualized what London Town must look like. Marilyn dressed us up like dolls and used her finest clothes from her wardrobe, and as she brushed our hair, I remember how beautiful both myself and Bulbul looked. Even the mirror was surrounded by a gold frame. We sat in the fancy chairs fit for the Queen of England herself.

'Marilyn said, "Now we are ready so let's go meet with Mr Tom. Are you girls hungry? It's dinner time now."

'"Oh yes, please," we both answered in harmony.

'Mr Tom was nowhere to be seen. Marilyn said, "I will go find him in the bar." We could see her walking through the patrons, asking, "Have you seen my Tom?" As she went from side to side, she returned and said, "I will check with the reception desk to enquire as to his whereabouts or find out if he had departed from the hotel."

'She rang the bell on the desk as a young lady behind the counter arrived. "Do you know where my fiancé is? Has he left the hotel?" said Marilyn.

'"Oh yes, ma'am. She was informed by the receptionist that two gentlemen had come to the hotel. They asked for Mr Tom, they spoke for a while, and he said they had urgent business to attend to, and he left the hotel with them. Mr Tom left this message in the room sixteen pigeonhole for your attention," she said as she retrieved it and handed it over to her.

'Marilyn ripped open the envelope and unfolded the one-paged note. Oh no, she looked very worried and franticly glanced around the multitude of people standing outside in front of the hotel entrance doors. But much to her disappointment, he had long gone and was nowhere to be seen. We walked right down the driveway, and Marilyn, Bulbul, and I stood, looking out the locked gates. I watched her flickering blue eyes as she peered out through the bars into the darkness. I noticed there was no let-up in the steady flow of people, animals, and transport of every description passing the hotel and travelling along the Mall Road in both directions. Many people had decided to call it a night and were already sleeping in groups on the bare sidewalk. Some babies cried in their mothers' arms, and the smell of urine filled the air.

'"Where has Mr Tom gone, Marilyn?" I asked.

'She replied, "I have no idea, but we shall find out later tonight."

'We slowly moved back towards the hotel entrance doors. She stared up at the clouds moving across the moonlit skies—an indication the monsoon season was on the way. "Oh, come on then. Our dinner will be getting cold."

'Marilyn joined us at the dinner table. We ate our meal in silence. Believe it or not, I cannot remember what the food was that night. I do not even think I finished it as I was so worried about her. But I still see her face as she sat staring across the room while she spun her fork around the plate with her right hand holding her head in position, clearly very unhappy with his leaving the hotel. I wanted to ask her a multitude of questions about her country. Looking at her current position, I decided not to.

'"Okay, sorry, girls," said Marilyn. "I think it is time for you two young ladies to get to bed." We stood up and headed under her escort to our room. "Good night and have a good sleep," said Marilyn. "And if you need me, I'm in my bedroom next door."

'Bulbul said, "Marilyn, do not worry. Mr Tom is a strong man and will be okay out there. He's probably on his way back already."

'"Thank you, Bulbul," replied Marilyn.

'After she departed, me and my sister tried to unravel the mystery as to why Mr Tom went out. But before long, we faded off into a deep sleep.

'On 15 August, the new India nation was first named the Union of India, but later that year, the government changed it to the 'Republic of India'. And as a vibrant, new country came into existence, many formal ceremonies were taking place across the divide.

'In the capital Delhi, Jawed Nehru was sworn into office. He assumed the position of prime minister. Moreover, when I heard the news that the Indians had also provided a seat to that English fellow Mountbatten as the viceroy and now the first governor general of India, I was mad with rage.

'The great majority of Indians remained calm, peaceful, and seemed to get on with the new independence they had just gained—a different story in the border areas where millions of Muslim, Sikh, and Hindu communities were forcibly relocated across the newly formed borders and many more were moved into refugee camps.

'Gandhi negotiated a deal with his counterpart and good friend Jinnah. They organized the exchange of Hindus and Muslims transited from Pakistan and India. Along their way, they had to cross over the newly formed border crossings by September 1947. Almost four million people in total moved to new areas.

'Up to now, there were three attempts to assassinate Gandhi. Then on 30 January 1948, during the prayer at 5:17 p.m., a gunman managed to get past security at Birla House gardens and fired three shots from a piston into Gandhi's body. He died later, surrounded by his closest family members and dignitaries. This gunman turned out to be a Hindu man. When the news spread, the two countries fell into a state of shock and horror.

'The newspapers wrote about Gandhi's calming presence and how he appeared to be able to manage and abate any communal tensions and tempers. It was said that was the very reason there was surprisingly less violence or disruptions across the board. But sadly, his death led to further upsurges in racial tensions.'

As Parveen spoke, there was an almost total silence in the air, only interrupted by the sound of crickets chattering in the still of the night. As she glanced around, she noticed many a tearful eye on the faces of her listeners.

'But really, more and more deviations were to come.' Parveen went on to say, 'During this period, the population of India was appropriately 300 million people. Poverty was rampant, and many were living hand to mouth. The nation's teacher—a humble man with a slender stature, a religious man, a guru of seventy-five years of servitude to his people—was now gone. Such a great loss at such an early period of our young country.

'The people still have shrines in their homes dedicated to him. Here in Pakistan and across the divide, our entire nation was totally shocked at what happened next. On 11 September 1948, hardly a year had passed since he was chosen for office, Jinnah, the governor general of Pakistan, died of natural causes. The entire country was in a state of shock with the passing of the nation's founding father. Since then, the day is a national holiday in his honor. In fact, Jinnah was born on 25 December, which is also the Christians' Christmas Day, which is also a national holiday.'

'Is that because of Jesus's birthday, it's a holiday?' asked one of the children.

'Oh no! It's only a coincidence that the two clashed on the same day. The national holiday is only because it's Jinnah's birthday. Us Christians, we are the lucky ones as you know we get the day off from work in the pits and the menfolk working in the kilns and farms celebrate Christmas.'

'Parveen, why do the two nations celebrate Independence Day on different days?' a clever little boy asked.

'It's because of time difference as Indian standard time is thirty minutes apart Pakistani standard time and Grange Meantime So the Pakistani people celebrate their independent on 14 August, and the Indian nation on 15 August. That's why!'

'Thank you, Auntie," the boy replied in gratitude.

Also, she said, 'The Indian state of Hyderabad remained in the hands of a prince. The Indian army were sent there by the government to pressure the royal prince to bring the province into under the new constitution.

'Let's go back to my story. Back then, in Fayette's Hotel, Lahore, Mama Braganza came into our hotel room, saying, "Rise and shine, my little darlings! It's a beautiful day outside, and you have slept right through to lunchtime. Make yourselves nice as Mr Tom and Marilyn are waiting to take you shopping in the famous Anarkali Bazaar.'

'"I've never heard of that bazaar before," I said to Mrs Braganza. As we got dressed, she went on to tell the story of Anarkali.

'Mrs Braganza stated, "The bazaar was named Anarkali after a young girl who worked at the Lahore mausoleum, thought to be a slave. Legend has it, she was buried alive by order of the Mughal emperor Akbar for having a sexual relationship with Prince Salem, the emperor's young son. The boy later became Emperor Salim Jahangir. Okay, Mr Tom and Marilyn intend to have you both measured up for new clothes in the Anarkali Bazaar. They will take you to the Lahore Zoological Gardens to see the wild animals—tigers, lions, elephants, monkeys."

'"Oh lovely," we said as we quickly washed and finished dressing ourselves and hurried along over to the garden where we met up with Mr Tom and Marilyn.

'Mr Tom greeted us on arrival into the garden. "Oh, girls, I am very sorry about not being around last night. But I intend to make it up to you three ladies today!" he said.

'"Oh no, it was okay, but we were worried about you and Marilyn."

'"Okay, let's go to the bazaar, Mr Tom, before this day is over."

'"But the girls have not eaten yet," Marilyn said.

'Tom replied, "We are going to have lunch near Ferozsons Bookstore on Mall Road. As I know you, Marilyn, you are going to update your library with some good technical books."

'Us girls never had sat in an automobile before.

'Mr Tom called his car. He joked while saying, "It comes in many colors black, black, and black." This confused both myself and my sister.

'Marilyn said, "It's Mr Tom's joke."

'"Okay! Let's drive on," he said to his driver. The rooftop was open fully as we cruised along down the Mall Road.

'Mr Tom asked, "Do you know what *the Mall* means?"

'Bulbul said but in the Punjabi language, "Its meaning is *oxen*."

'"Very good, girls."

Marilyn and Mr Tom glanced over at each other, smiling.

Mr Tom went on to say, "Long time ago, the Mall Road was used by farmers taking their products from farm to markets."

'Much to everyone's surprise, all the shops and restaurants were shuttered up, and looters were stealing anything they could get their hands on.

'Mr Tom shouted over to a shopkeeper, "Hi there! Can you please explain what's happening? Did you happen to see a couple of men hanging around here? They are supposed to meet me here on the corner." What is going on, enquired Mr Tom, to the shop keeper.

'"Oh! The Pakistani government intend to ban the sale of liquor and alcohol. I think they are going to ban smoking too!" said the shopkeeper.

'"No, sir," replied the shopkeeper. "Is it important?"

'"Oh no, maybe they went to the hotel. Anyways, thank you very much for the other information and bye," said Mr Tom.

'"Terrible tragedy," said Mr Tom. "At least there will be alcohol at the hotel. Let's go back and review the situation from there. Looking like lots of trouble and traffic building up around here."

'The short trip back to the hotel that normally took about fifteen minutes lasted almost one hour. Thousands upon thousands more people travelling on every sort of transportation had jammed up the road.'

Parveen continued while wiping her tears from her eyes, 'The great division of our humble nation (India) had a deviating effect on the ancient communities and its territories consisting of many nomadic people. At that time, many different ethnic communities from a multitude of religious backgrounds were caught up in bloody civil disarray on both sides of the newly marked out international boundaries. The split caused families and relatives to be separated as they struggled to escape the violence that immediately followed the British departure. Entire communities were set upon, murdered, and houses were torched and ransacked. Whatever personal possessions they had were stolen, and livestock taken away.'

Parveen's old eyes were flashing from side to side as she paused and said, 'Look here to where we are now sitting. This is our homeland in the desert, with plenty of space for everyone. Did you know it was mentioned on the radio that the Indian Thar Desert had become the most densely populated desert in the world?

'After partition, the mixed population density was stated to be more than eighty-five or ninety persons per square kilometre. The Pakistani area of Sindh province was settled mainly by indigenous tribal communities (Parks-Kohl's) and a variety of other internally displaced people. The (Parks-Kohl's) are a sight for sore eyes and a colorful spectrum that still manage to scrap up an existence out across the desert.

'My people,' she said, 'taking ownership, remained deeply attached to a rich traditional culture, with very invigorating folklore stories.'

She went on to say how she loved the romantic songs and, in many cases, the extremely sad songs they sang.

'The heritage derived from Sufism and Hinduism stated that even though the Sindh province was mainly populated by these two religions, the province was given to the Islamic Republic of Pakistan in 1947. The transition occurred with minimum of tensions, in comparison with that of Punjab and Kashmir provinces.

'Yes, I can't forget either our fabulous Sindhi male folk dancers as they performed dances majestically from below the highest sand dunes for funerals, weddings, and during the festive seasons.

Others within our community have a rich heritage of skills and talents that they passed down from grandfathers to fathers and on to sons and daughters.

'Military hardware left behind by the British was distributed amongst the newly established Pakistani defense forces. As time went by and a sufficient type of order was created in both countries, law and order started to take hold. Jinnah managed to calm down the now Muslim majority in Pakistan, and likewise, Gandhi did the same over the border in India with the multicultural communities.' She stated, 'It had taken what seemed forever to settle down after the last British ships departed for the United Kingdom.

'Everyone and everything throughout the land was still up for grabs. The Pakistani leader and the newly formed government established the Pakistani army, navy, and air force. Both defense forces and armies set up defensive positions along the Mountbatten 'line of control' between the two new nations. Networks of roads, railways, and bridges on the Radcliffe borderline were dismantled, and fences erected. This program finalized the partition design and created an uneasy peace.'

Parveen told the group of listeners that in the Punjab, where the new borderlines divided the Sikh and Hindi regions in half, there were the most violent crimes and the most bloodshed. Body counts were not available as hardly any official figures gathered because, across the divide, there was a total breakdown of administrative committees. And therefore, the normal functional gathering of statistics simply didn't exist. But local estimates indicate the number of deaths to be in the region of 1.5 million people.

Moreover, across the divides, Muslim clerics, Christians, and many other faiths and missionaries set about organizing themselves and maneuvered their resources to take advantage of the situation and to gain grounds by converting as many people within a short time frame.

Alongside this, well-organized criminals and their networks of underground agents tuck advantage of the situations. The innocent; displaced; internal refugees with widows, single females, and poor uneducated women were forced to marry rich landlords and businessmen. Thousands more were sold into slavery. Children were taken away from their families or kidnapped while running errands, such as fetching water or tending to their animals as they watched them on patches of vegetation. Many of these women and children were taken to be forced to work within a variety of unpaid positions throughout the land, such as sex trade; sweatshops making clothes, textiles, and hand-knitted carpets; or bonded laborers in brick kilns.

Parveen said, 'You are already taware our father's dad who was my grandfather. He derived from Portugal. He was a Christian who went to Goa as a lay missionary. After some time, he became a stationmaster. They called us Anglo-Indian. My dad had good education and could speak a few languages as his father always insisted on his kids to study hard. I expect that is the main reason he was given a posting as stationmaster.'

'Were the other stationmasters Anglo-Indian too?' asked one of the women in the group.

'Oh yes,' she replied. 'The entire railway staff, including the train engineers, were Anglo Indian. If you remember when I told you how we managed to escape from Kamoke, it felt strange how we were able to survive while everyone around us was getting murdered.

'The British employed mostly European professional personnel, such as civil engineers and locomotive engineers. Most of the contracts for railway track construction went to British companies, and the general labor force were normally from India. A shortage of hardware and parts started to arise as most of this came from the United Kingdom. The Raj built two different modern railway systems, one to the east and the other in the west of the country.

'During the war, the railway workshops were turned into munitions factories. As the war progressed, shortages of parts and repair of existing components for the trains became harder to maintain. Adding to this, many of the carriages and best locomotives were shipped out of India to the Middle East, which created a shortage in local supply, and services were cut to many outreached locations. After 1947, the two main systems were nationalized by the Indian government operated in a haphazard fashion, hardly capable of providing a reliable service to the general commuters.

'It was said afterwards that, amazingly, most of the Anglo-Indians and Christians seemed to survive or appeared to be spared by Muslim, Sikh, and Hindu in fighting. Even our sacred places such as churches, shrines, and houses belonging to Anglo-Indians and Christians were hardly touched. I expect they could distinguish by our dress code being so different from the rest, standing out in a crowd, possibly saving our lives.

'For a lot of these Hindu and Muslim women and children, some would try escape to return home, only to be found by their captives and forced to return and live out their lives in exile within their own country, and in most cases, this was done by their own family members or neighbors for one reason or the other, but mainly because of severity of poverty, hunger, and survival reasons. Look at the time,' Parveen said. 'I've talked right through the night.'

As Parveen departed to her house that very same morning, she noticed the Malik who owned the brick kiln. He received two visitors to his land from the Pakistani Environmental Protection Authority Some children greeted them as they climbed out of their driver-driven vehicle.

'What do you want down here, mister?' asked one of the children.

'We are here on official business to meet the Malik Saab (gentleman),' one of the men replied.

'That's the Malik over there. Okay, sir! And he is coming over to meet you, it seems,' said another child.

A minute passed by before both parties came together on the side of the dusty, unsurfaced, windy track, just opposite the brick-batching pit. A group of onlookers gathered not too far away. Parveen also was there and stood amongst them.

'What's going on?' an inquisitive old man asked as he leaned on top of his shovel.

'The Malik seems to be discussing our shanty village setup with them.'

'Look, they are pointing in our direction again.'

The group of men continued in deep discussion as they approached the edge of the pit and were well within earshot. Per common practice of hospitality and customs throughout the country, when guests arrive, the local community provided the guests with a place to sit, water, and if available, hot tea. Parveen's house was closed; therefore, she provided two charpoys beds for the guest and the Malik to sit on under the shade of her only little tree. Moreover, she brought out the family rug for them to sit on.

Parveen listened to the Malik explain about the livelihoods of the general population of the desert area. she noticed how most of the workers had stopped working and had moved up close enough to listen intensely to every word of the conversation between the Malik and the government officials and get the gist of what was said. It was understood as not good news for the entire community. It was clear from the mumbling throughout group that they were not happy and began to have worried looks on their faces. They whispered to one another what possibly could these men want.

The Malik was also overheard saying, 'the main occupations of the people in this desert are agriculture, animal husbandry. Yes, as you have noticed, there are a few brick kilns here and there the far fewer than the local construction industry required. Also, I'm sure you are aware it's because of the insufficient quality of good soils available out across the semi desert.'

The Malik continued by saying, 'As you people are aware, The Thar Desert areas consist mostly of barren outreaches of partly productive lands, and sand dunes are covered with thorny short bushes and clumps of wild grasses. In most cases, the unhospitable ridges are topped off by the most amazingly high sand dunes with their irregular shapes and sizes. Pointing out across the landscape, you can see how they are lined up roughly in parallel lines with deep sheltered valleys hidden in between. Some of the larger dunes tower in heights of up to fifty metres.

'Whenever it rains, the valleys become wet enough to grow rain-fed crop cultivation, and when not cultivated, they yield an abundance of one-metre-high grasses. Many local inhabitants harvest this grass. they take them to the local markets and sell it for roof construction on traditional mud housing or other uses, such as flat screening for village compound fences. The fence provides privacy for the womenfolk behind the boundary fence and safety for the extended families living within.

'The salinity of the subsoil and shortage of portable water make it hard to sustain a healthy lifestyle for both man and beast alike. But even so, one cannot but admire this majestic terrain that is rather picturesque in its own setting. Life is difficult but goes on, and generations of Sindhi families continue to endure and scratch out a meagre existence from the desert soil in a variety of livelihoods—for instance, animal husbandry of camels, donkeys, goats, and sheep, firewood gathering for sale in markets, cottage industry weaving baskets and other traditional handmade crafts. Just lately, we have added Pakistani and international tourism to the list.'

One of the officials replied, 'Do you get many tourists through here then?'

'Oh yes, I am also keen to build a small hotel or guest house as I have been watching these activities with great interest. I don't really want to spend all my life in farming. I am considering moving to Karachi and invest in hiring a farm manager to run the whole show for me.'

The Malik said while looking around at his property, 'I suppose I'm one of the lucky farmers with sufficient quantity of good soil in my possession. Therefore, we are capable of manufacturing a reasonable quantity of high-quality bricks, but I must say, the quality drops off a little during the monsoon season. Again, given our location here and proximity to the Punjab, we get a fair share of the rains.

'But in the last twenty or thirty years, with the ever-increasing expansion of the human and animal populations, the natural resources are diminishing. Back then, we used the sugar-cane waste materials to feed the fire in the kiln, which helps me keep our operation cost to a minimum.

'Another good factor was our in-house residential dwellers brick-kiln workers and farmhands, provided cheap labor costs. Originally, we were using wood from the desert, but now it has to be gathered further and further away as the supplies dwindle.

'Another consideration was the labor and transportation costs were tremendously higher to bring it back here. We only grow sugar cane in the fields for up to five years then rest the fields for one year in order to let the soil rejuvenate. Otherwise, there is a chance of overworking the soil. In many cases, it becomes selenic, and nothing will grow. This is when we have to order in the wood from the desert.

'Back when my father and grandfather were alive—peace be upon their souls—before partition, the lands produced healthier crops. Everything was more sustainable and abundant. That was when the family decided to build up an irrigation system. Up to then, most of the crops were selected haphazardly as seasonable varieties of rain-fed types. Some years when we had little rain or the fields were not prepped on time, the crop yield was much lesser.

'That tube-well pump house standing over there was established by our aging grandfather. At first, it was seldom used as no one could start it. I remember my father shouted, "Why did we spend so much money on the construction when all it does is stand idle?" Until one day in springtime, the new gardener arrived from Lahore to work on our farm. He had a vast working experience in diesel pumps. Since then, it's been his job to service it, and he keeps it running smoothly.'

The Malik laughed and said, 'The gardener calls it his baby. I remember it was around 1960 when diesel became available throughout rural Pakistan on a vast scale. Most rural holdings make good usage of the advancement in the new technologies. And with the added welcomed advice from the friendly governmental agriculturists and ergonomists, we continue with their assistance, and they come here regularly to check such things as the soil samples, seed multiplication. They introduced a wide variety of suitable crop options for this area. Mostly, they brought the samples to Karachi University for undergraduate students to prepare the tests. Later, the field staff would return and provide technical know-how during the implementation period.

'But now with the population boom, perhaps this has led to improper control of grazing and extensive cultivation resulting into the weakening of vegetation and natural resources that added to the decrease in accessibility to water.'

The officials stated, 'Yes, you are right, Malik Saab. This very increase of human and livestock populations in the desert has further weakened the natural ecosystem, resulting in the degradation to the fertility of the soils, mainly because of cutting too many wild trees, Halifax, grasses, and other natural vegetation.'

The officials went on to say aloud, 'The Thar Desert continues to expand outwards. Sand is constantly moving as during the dry summer season, it is dry as the wind blows out across the desert, encroaching on neighboring fertile soils and agricultural lands. It has, in effect, sped up the advancing desert so much in a lot of places, covered boundary walls of properties as well as blocking of roads, covered up railway lines—just to mention a few of the concerns the government are trying to curtail. Moreover, the government plans to tackle the erosion issues with the introduction of buffer zones constructed in selected high-risk zones as a kind of conservative control measure along by this wasteland to slow down the desert's advancement.

'In order to implement this project,' he went on to say, 'the government has planned to reclaim the pits and refill the holes to demolish these brick kilns and the cluster of shanty villages and relocate these people onto a different area then build a massive sand barrier and plant millions of trees. This will slow down the advancing desert sands.'

'You are an educated man, Malik Saab, and I'm sure you are also aware that you are trespassing on the Pakistani government state lands.' The officials went on to say, 'Okay, look here!' as he stretched out a large topographical map across Parveen's colored family rug.

Pointing to a highlighted yellow line, he said, 'Here is where your property line falls and ends, and there is where the government owned land and demarcation line begin.

'Do you know that if the government officials discovered that you were using the government designated lands to manufacture bricks and make a profit on their land, I'm sure, Malik Saab, they would consider making you and your family pay back a hefty huge amount of money in taxes and other charges. Surely, all your good efforts on the farm would probably not cover the entire costs. Then what?

'And furthermore, I expect they would calculate the bill to cover the duration right back to the very year of partition in 1947. I suggest the best advice we can give you would be to comply with the governmental master plan for this area and cut your losses of the brick kiln. Surely, you are sufficiently wealthy to continue to make a healthy living from your crops. But imagine, if the consequences of that very same sand continued to invade your fertile soils then what? It's a case of necessity for the betterment of the entire community and Pakistan.'

The Malik, for the first time in his life, felt vulnerable and hopeless. He looked distress and flustered as he glanced around at the now silent group of muddy faces. He thought, *What is going to become of all these people? I will not be able to provide work. There is no other soil suitable to produce high-quality bricks.*

The older men and boys approached the Malik and, in a humble way, shook his hand and rubbed his two feet before wandering back to their tasks they were doing prior to the arrival of the two government officials some four hours ago as they discussed and tried to absorb the information shuffled away while looking back to the Malik with compassion and sympathy.

The Malik, sitting across, said to the two men, 'Let's see where this will all end up. The new government are too busy to really be concerned about this area. I will wait and see where to act and will go to Karachi soon to follow up on this story as I have many contacts in the different departments there. Hopefully, today's exercise was all in vain.'

Parveen started to say, 'Hey, you there! We have lived here for most of our lives! Best you go pack up your belongings and head back to your fancy offices in Karachi and please forget about this useless project of yours. Yeah, go clean up your own backyard first and leave us alone to take care of our affairs. We definitely can sort out this so-called erosion problem in our constructive manner and own way. We will plant millions of trees to stop the erosion and make Pakistan beautiful.' She shouted. 'Pakistan Zindabad (Long Live Pakistan)!'

This response was appreciated by the many people listening. As they all joined in repeating the slogan 'Pakistan Zindabad (Long Live Pakistan)', The two officials looked at each other. They appeared frightened, and as one rolled up the map, he instructed the driver to start up the engine of their vehicle in order to make a hasty escape if the need arose.

'Calm down, people,' said the Malik. 'Please come to my house to discuss this further over lunch.'

"Thank you, Malik, but we need to be heading back to Karachi to report on our findings here. I expect you will receive an official letter related to our site visit. You are right. It may take a very long time for any action to build the sand barrier, especially this far east and close to the Indian border.'

The men shook hands with the Malik before climbing into the back seat of their vehicle.

It was obvious she had the backup from the group standing around her as they chanted, 'Long live Parveen!'

The Malik, for once, looked helpless and scratched his head in silence. As the three-gentleman walked back towards the government vehicle that was now parked a shorter distance away than before the meeting, they all stood there and watched them climb into the vehicle and waited for them to drive away, leaving them standing in a cloud of dust.

Shortly after the government officials departed out of sight and over the horizon, the Malik, raising his hand, quelling the situation, said, 'Please, Parveen, please don't be disrespectful of these two gentlemen. They are only doing their governmental job. It's not their fault, and I will try stop this from happening myself through my contacts in the Karachi or Hyderabad offices. I really have to do something fast in order for the planning committees to cancel at least part of the sand barrier. I expect it will be a costly exercise, and I will need to pay for it somehow.'

'How will you do this?' enquired Parveen.

'Did you not just hear what I said?' replied the Malik. 'I will go meet with them in Karachi myself and hopefully prevent any evictions or even the construction of this man-made sand dunes and whatever structures they wish to push on us. Please, now go back to your work,' said the Malik.

Parveen paused for a moment to catch her breath. As if this land problem was not enough to handle. On top of this, my daughter-in-law Asahi was heavily pregnant. Like everyone else, she was expected to continue working with the rest of the women and children in the clay pit. It was a normal functional day for her, along with a variety of other chores, such as

1. foot-stomping clay into a putty-like substance by adding water to the soil;
2. continuing by pressing the softened clay into wet timber-frame moulds by hand;

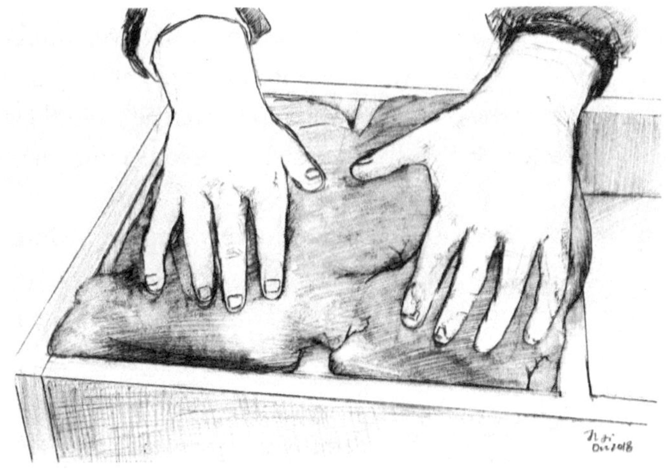

LADY MOULDING BRICKS BY HAND

3. then laying the bricks out on the ground to be sun-baked;
4. carrying the sun-baked bricks up the steep embankment when the bricks had consolidated;
5. placing the bricks into specially arranged stacks in the kiln for baking;
6. transferring the bricks by manhandling them into trucks to complete the process; and
7. on top of all these tasks, doing most of the family chores, such as preparing meals, cleaning the house, washing clothes, fetching water, and collecting firewood.

Asahi was beleaguered as she fell on her back in the clay—distraught, dehydrated, sick, and exhausted. She began to call out to one of the other women to run get help. While putting her hand down between her legs, she noticed her water had just broken. She struggled to catch her breath through every contraction.

Her husband Mushtaq quickly approached to assist her and, feeling helpless, shouted out, 'Please! Somebody go and get the midwife from her house over there.'

His wife Asahi said, 'Honey! It is too late. The baby is coming, and I can't stop it.'

Their two young daughters Rani, four, and Neela, five, stood watching, froze to the spot where they were standing, squinted, and held on to each other as they observed the blood-covered head emerged from their mother's body. The birth was not a difficult one, and before long, the baby had arrived.

Their father Mushtaq looked flustered and confused while shouting out, 'It's a boy!' and said, 'Allah be praised!'

He quickly ushered Rani and Neela away and out of their house to find their grandma.

The midwife arrived after some time. She began fussing around and complained, 'That baby was not supposed to be here until next month,' she stated. 'It's not my inaccuracy. He is premature, and I still will need to be compensated no matter what. Allah be acclaimed.'

She washed the boy's little skinny body. She said, looking down to where Asahi was lying on the bed, 'Are you aware your son is way underweight and too small? I don't think he is probably going to survive more than a few weeks in this extreme heat.'

Asahi looked concerned and asked her to stop saying such things. 'You are going to put an evil spell on him if you continue to say things like that. I think you better leave my home now.'

'Where's my money then?' she shouted.

Mushtaq, hearing the argument, entered the room. 'Why are you shouting and upsetting my wife?'

'She's not going to pay me!' replied the old midwife.

'Neither am I, so get out,' said Mushtaq, 'as you didn't do anything, only wash the baby.'

'I'm not leaving until I'm paid,' she replied.

Mushtaq opened the door and pointed his finger outside. 'Go now while you can!' he said.

In an instant, she ran out, saying, 'Wait until my husband finds out. He will come down here and get what I am rightly due from you.'

'Let's see about that,' Mushtaq said and slammed the door closed in a fit of temper.

'Maybe we should have paid her,' Asahi said.

Mushtaq said, 'Don't worry. I'll probably pass her house later and talk with her and her husband. Hopefully, he will make her see some sense. But whatever the outcome, she will not be getting any money for the birth of the baby. I can assure you of that. Also, for good luck, I will bring a box of traditional candies.'

Asahi laughed. 'She's losing her marbles. Maybe it's time for her to retire from midwifery.'

Next morning, Mushtaq surprised Asahi with the news. He had already named the baby boy during the night as his mother slept. A circumcision ceremony was also implemented. Imran lay crying for his mom to try to breastfeed him to give him another bottle of camel milk as a feed.

She was not impressed on hearing he went ahead and performed it while she slept. 'I was afraid he might die, and if he died before he was made a Muslim, he would not go to paradise. I didn't think you would mind as you knew he was to become Muslim.'

'But you know how much I like celebrating everything, and I'm not upset. I am happy for Imran,' said Asahi.

Asahi, still in bed, lay there with sad eyes peering across at him as Imran struggled to attract her attention. She had lost a lot of blood during the birth.

'Come on, my darling son.' He picked the baby up and gently placed him into the bed beside his mother. 'There now, my little son. Your mommy's going to breastfeed you.'

Asahi replied, 'I don't think I've got any milk, but let me try. She seemed ever so surprised as the baby managed to suckle and had a fill then drifted off into a peaceful sleep in her arms.

Imran's father sighed, wondering how they were going to make ends meet with another child as he counted to three using his fingers to get the total figure.

He said to his wife, 'That's three children we have! No more.'

She agreed with Mushtaq with a smirk grin on her face, and he left the room to head off to work. Within moments, Mushtaq stuck his head in the door again and sent a kiss to her in her direction.

She raised her hand to catch it and laughed as she smacked it to her lips.

'Goodbye, dear,' she said, and he went outside into the early morning sunshine.

Asahi watched him through the tiny window as he prepared the camel by placing the halter and bit into her mouth before walking her out through the gate. He waved a final farewell in through the window and briskly headed out into the desert.

***

In May 1987, Imran was seven years of age when baby boy Caleb was born. The village had a new midwife. The old midwife died shortly after she left them that day when Imran was born, that seemed a very long years ago. Asahi looked across to her husband Mushtaq who appeared disappointed. He was trying hard to avoid eye contact.

But when she asked him what was the matter with him, he stood up from where he was sitting just outside on the tiny veranda. He peered in through the window, holding up four fingers to indicate that's the last one. But Asahi smiled back in a defiant sort of manner.

Asahi passed a comment, saying, 'As if it's my fault. Don't forget you are half the blame too.'

He didn't answer her back but continued to sulk. But as many days passed, Mushtaq finally got over it, and before long, he joined her upon the bed to play with little Caleb. During the early days, Imran felt strange as up to now, he was the baby of the house. He felt left out as the new baby got more attention from his mom, dad, and now his grandmas (Parveen and his two eldest sisters).

However, Imran still loved his baby brother, cared for and looked after him day and night. By the time Caleb was approximately eighteen months old, crawling around on all fours, he followed him everywhere. He was just starting to walk. So Imran managed to carry him around, hanging off his hip. Besides this, he made sure to feed Caleb by pushing every type of food into his mouth. Moreover, this was done under the close watchful eyes of their grandma.

Imran enjoyed the companionship he shared as all three of them sat up on the charpoy bed under the shade of the one small tree in their garden. On this day, Grandma (Parveen) was busy cutting up ladyfingers and string green peas she had harvested from the family vegetable patch. She hummed a popular Punjabi song. Leaning forward on the bed, she pushed a few freshly popped peas into her eldest grandson's mouth.

'Eat them uncooked, boy. There are plenty of them for everyone. They taste better, and they are good for you.'

Imran replied, 'Gee, thanks, Grandma,' and went on to ask her, 'Where is my grandpa?'

'He is up in heaven.'

Imran said, 'He is in heaven. Yeah, that's where he is!'

And she raised her two hands towards the skies. But then Imran changed the subject very quickly with small talk to avoid the subject.

'Whatever happened to him? How come I never met him? And how do you know he is in heaven? Did Allah tell you he was in heaven?' Imran said.

'Imran, please stop with all the questions. I'm getting very upset.'

'Sorry, Grandma. I don't want to make you feel sad. It's okay,' said Imran.

***

A year passed. The day after Imran's eight birthday, he was having a stubborn type of day. As he stood in the centre of the pit, he moaned and complained to his mother, saying, 'Why, Momma (Asahi)? Why do we have to do this work for the Malik Saab?'

'He sees us as uneducated and illiterate peasants, Asahi,' his mother replied.

Imran glanced out across the dirt track towards the Malik's mansion surrounded by mango and banana trees. He also observed the sugar-cane crops as they stood tall as far as the eye could see across the land. He noticed that the Malik's sons were swimming in the tube-well water pond.

Imran asked Parveen, 'Hey, Grandma, can I go play over there with those boys? And maybe they will let me swim in the pond too with them,' as he jumped around in anticipation of a positive response from her.

'No,' Parveen replied. 'This is not possible. They are upper class, and we are just untouchables.'

Imran eyed her as he asked, 'Why do they call us untouchable?'

'Because in the towns and cities, our traditional tasks include the disposal of dead animals and manual cleaning of sewers, sweeping roads and cleaning—'

She couldn't finish her statement because of his interruptions as he went on to say, 'But I'm so hot, and I don't care what they call us.' Imran, in disobedience and in defiance, kicked at the ground that raised a cloud of bright red dust that encircled his grandma.

He shouted out, 'But they are boys just like me!' Imran ran off in the direction of the tube-well pond.

Parveen stumbled to her feet from a crouched position and screamed out after him, 'Imran, please come back right now!'

He glanced back over his shoulder but soon reached the pond.

'Hello, can I play with you boys and swim in the pond too?' Imran asked the Malik's sons.

'Papa, Papa, help! Please, Papa, help! A peasant boy from the dirty brick kiln is on our private property!' one of the boys shouted out in great distress and with a disgusted look across his wet face. 'Go away! Get away from here! Papa!'

Imran didn't understand why he's not welcomed there.

The other brother shouted too, pointing in the direction for Imran to leave. The Malik appeared out of the house with a shotgun in hand and shouted, 'Get out of here or I will!'

Before he could finish his sentence, Imran ran scared as fast as hell back towards the pit and into the safety of his grandma's arms. To pacify the Malik from a distance, Parveen pretended to beat Imran on the bottom with her flat hand.

Both Imran and the rest of the brick-kiln children workers watched as the Malik and his sons went back into their house.

Parveen said to Imran and all the other children, 'Let that be a lesson to you all! Don't go there, any of you, do you understand?'

'Yes, Grandma!' he replied.

'Now get back to work. We need to make two hundred more bricks today to break even with our quotas.'

To change the mood of things, Parveen said, 'Hey, Imran, do you know where we get this water we are using to stomp and mix with the clay to make these bricks?'

'No,' Imran replied.

'It's the Malik's water from his tube well.'

'Oh yes,' Imran said. 'It falls into the pit from up top over there. Am I right, Grandma?'

'Yes, very good, Imran.' She clapped him on the shoulder.

He smiled back at her with contentment and said, 'But why isn't it falling? And there isn't any coming today.'

'Because it only arrives over there a few days after he switches on his diesel generator. The water comes up from far below the surface of the ground. Then first, it goes into the tube-well pond where his two sons were swimming today. Then the water goes into a series of irrigation channels, zigzags throughout his property to provide water to a variety of vegetables and plants, long before it's our turn to receive our share into the little waterfall over there in the corner.'

'Oh, thanks for explaining that,' Imran said. 'It's a lot of water network and scheming before we get a share. Do we have to pay for this water?' Imran asked his grandma.

'No, the water, the pit, these bricks, the kilns are all belonging to the Malik,' Grandma replied.

'He's very rich then,' Imran said as he scanned the area around his house while absorbing all the information he just learnt. 'I hate work,' Imran said as he lowered himself down while he was slapping the soft mud into the wooden-framed brick mould. His mother assisted him by straightening it into the rows with the already cast bricks.

His mother (Asahi) did her best to encourage him to settle down. 'Do you want a drink of water?' she asked Imran.

'No, Mother (Asahi). Thank you anyway.' He stopped to look across towards the Malik's house, saying, 'I probably won't ever go there again.'

Shortly after, Imran stood up as he could hear laughter coming from the Malik's mansion, followed by the sound of a car engine starting up.

'Where are they going, Mother?' he inquisitively asked her.

'The boys will be going to school,' Imran's mother replied.

'Can't I go there too, Mommy?'

'No, we can't afford it. Maybe someday, maybe someday.' She sighed. 'Come on, Imran,' she said to him. 'Let's see how many bricks you can make before we eat.'

'When are we going to eat, Mommy?'

'Imran, shut up, please! You are doing my head in.' She sighed. 'Stop!' Imran replied, 'Okay, Mommy!'

Grandma (Parveen) cleverly stated, 'This year the rains haven't played their vital role in our lives yet as water deposits and levels in the tubas (small ponds) are very low and murky. This water is vital for our very survival. Because it hasn't come, the community is short of water for drinking, washing, and other purposes.'

She continued, saying, 'These tubas are the only source of water for our animals and humans living in most of the desert areas. Unlike the

Punjab, up there, the water tables are well within reach. So there are wells and hand pumps everywhere. But down here, whenever it rains, it soaks away through the fine sand too deep to reach it. For this reason, the greater portion of our population has to live a nomadic existence. When a tuba becomes too dry, they are forced to move to a new location and set up a home around the water-filled tuba.'

Imran asked his grandma, 'How do you know everything?'

She said, 'I have seen many things throughout my life. When I was young, life was very different. The British ruled our country. They were lovely people if they had remained in our country. We would not be doing this. Their mighty infrastructure and wisdom encouraged everyone to get on and live together in harmony. My dad went off to fight for them. When he was killed there, officers came to our humble little house and gave my widowed mother a few hundred rupees and a service medal. We were so proud to see how she wore it over her heart while sweeping the railway platforms,' Parveen said and stared out in the open desert.

The boy, holding on to her hands, gently squeezed and massaged them as she struggled to control them from trembling. He asked, 'Grandma, do you miss your momma?'

'Oh yes, every day and night, I look up into the heavens, and when I see a shooting star, I pray for her and my daddy too. I'm not even sure if she is alive and well. It would be great to find out if she made it over the new border to India back in 1947.'

'Maybe she is still alive and remarried,' Imran said.

'No, she would be very old. But my brother could be alive living in India.'

'And maybe he got married too,' Imran said.

'When my sister Bulbul and I first came here to Sindh, we had nowhere to live. The Malik's father—Lord, have mercy on his dead soul—lent me and Bulbul enough money to build a one-roomed housing unit which was constructed with a combination of straw and thin wood sticks or strips of bark from the hardwood trees. Most of the money went on the transportation of materials, and the tradesman who built it got the rest. The first stormy season proved disastrous when we came back from work. One day we found it had been blown away.' She sighed.

'Then the Malik was kind enough and lent us more money. This time, we could build two rooms and a small veranda, and luckily, it's still standing together today.

TYPICAL REMOTE SINDHI VILLAGE SETTING

'My sister Bulbul and I, in our free time from work, cast every sun-baked brick for the house with our own bare hands.' Parveen pointed across at the double wooden door. 'We got the door and two tiny shattered windows from a widow who was moving away to live in Karachi after her husband died in search of a better life. She sold them to us in order to get money for the journey. She seemly had a brother who owned a bakery, so her hope was he would let her work baking bread in his shop. I often think of how she faired out. The other women said she must have made it safely as we never heard anything more since she left here.

'With all the building materials available on the plot of land for the house in between our work, with a bit of help here and there from a couple of the other ladies, after a couple of months, we managed to build it ourselves. It's not perfect, but it's been our home ever since. Yeah, the good old days.

'Few days before the rainy season, we were able to move in. I remember the excitement and tears of happiness on the face of my sister Bulbul, and over the days, we acted as if we were rich like the Malik. How good it was to own a home and have safety of being able to close the door at night and cuddle up in bed together.

'But within a couple of weeks, our happiness changed to sadness as the Malik's son started to take advantage and opportunities upon himself while binge-drinking with a few of his rich young friends. He must have been seventeen or eighteen years of age then. So while his father was away on business trips to Karachi or overseas, he would attack both myself and my sister for sex, and that's when Bulbul met her final destiny.'

Parveen said before weeping and breaking down then stumbling out across the uneven surface of the ground and crossing over rows of freshly cut bricks, 'I briskly walked away, briefly looking back towards the boy to ensure he left me alone.'

To change the subject, she said, 'Did you know we still haven't managed to earn enough to pay for the house? Seems like we never will as we get deeper and deeper into debt, with more cash payments for weddings, funerals, and general-living necessities all borrowed from the Malik. He charges very high rate. In return, all our family must work to pay him back. It's a vicious cycle. Yeah, the bonded laborers can't seem to break free from this life. Maybe someday soon! Hopefully, I can see it through before I die too. Nothing has been more personal or as compelling as the death of my younger sister.'

Mother (Asahi) said, 'We are luckily working to keep a roof over our heads and enough food to eat in the table. Yes, it's our destiny here and only natural for us to work as brick moulders and sometimes farm laborers here in Sindh. We are proud to be Pakistani. It's God's will, no matter how small a contribution we are making to our country. Every little help's build up our nation.'

To this statement, everyone present shouted, 'Pakistan! Long Live Pakistan!'

'Yes, I also know the very hard, long, tiring hours from sun up to sun down. But we are better off as we get Christmas and other festivals and national holidays off work.' She continued to say, 'We also get Sunday mornings off for Catholic religious studies too.'

Parveen joined in, 'It's extremely hard work. Look at my hands,' as she hunched over on her bended knees and held her hands outstretched. Parveen's withered face really showed her age, and every wrinkle her extremely hard life.

'We get up every morning every day,' she said. 'We put one foot in front of the other. We have to keep going. The unbreakable spirit of the kiln-working community of Pakistan is amazing. That is who we are.'

Another woman asked her to say, 'Hey, Parveen, how long have you worked here?'

'I can't remember how many years it was since my sister and I were sold off by my very own handsome stranger Mr Tom and Marilyn back in 1947. My mother was right—don't trust anyone.

'Believe me, we were very lucky to escape with our lives from Kamoke District. It's hard to know how we survived as we had to stumble across hundreds of dead bodies.

'But we truly believed we were safe with Marilyn and Mr Tom and at the hotel. That very night, when we were asleep in our Fayette's Hotel room on that last night, there was a loud crash in our room. We were awoken to find two men and Mr Tom standing by our beds. They tied us up and placed a piece of tape across our mouths. We were trying to escape, but the men were too strong. I remember how they passed us out through the window and bundled us into the trunk of Mr Tom's automobile. We screamed to no avail. The vehicle drove for a long time before it came to a stop.

'We were taken out of the car and put into the back of a truck. There were many other women inside. It was difficult to find a place to settle as a lot of the women pushed others away from their claimed spaces. There were some tied up along the side panels of the truck in a standing position. They relieved themselves. The smell of vomit, urine, excrement, and stench of soiled clothing made it very hard to breath. As we travelled down south towards Multan, one of the older women died alongside us in the crowded truck.

'Occasionally, the driver and his helpers would stop to throw the dead bodies off unto the roadside. The old lady was the first one. We never saw any of the towns after Multan as the captors placed a large canvas over the top of the truck to hide its inside. They told us if any of us made noise, they would take us out and cut our throats.

'At the Sukkur Barrage, the truck again stopped and dropped off some of the sick women and girls. They were left to fend for themselves on the side of the road. The roadway was not surfaced with asphalt at that time, so as we departed, the truck covered them in a cloud of dust. The remainder of us were permitted to wash ourselves in the Indus River, a few miles away from where they were dropped off. The water was very cold, and many of the women caught a cold. Even though the sun was shining, because of the wind from the moving truck and wet clothes, it was cold. But they were afraid to cough in case the captors would drop them off too.

'Eventually, we made it to a farmyard. There was businessmen and slave traders, and we were auctioned off. I supposed we were luckier than some of the other women as the Malik bought Bulbul, myself, and a few others. I never saw the other girls. But rumors say they were taken to the farms and only worked in the fields.

'But the Malik—peace be upon him—was a kind man, and with the help of our prayers, he helped us dodge death yet once again. In hindsight,' Grandma (Parveen) said, 'I wondered what my life would be like now if they hadn't been sold into bonded labor and taken here to work for the Malik's family. Oh yes! I think I was fifteen years old.'

'So that makes you fifty-four years old. You are still a young woman.'

'But look at me. I've aged terribly because of the rough lifestyle I've had to endure ever since I got here to the Sindhi desert. I'm the luckier of the two.' She remembered gazing out across the stacks of freshly moulded bricks as a dark plumb of smoke billowed out from the steel chimneys on top of the bull-pit kiln.

'Why is that?' the woman asked.

'Well, my younger sibling Bulbul died in his bedroom, you know. He raped her. I imagined it was because of her screaming so much, and he was drunk. But that was before he got married and settled down with his fancy wife.

'He used to get madly drunk and take one or two of us young girls to his father's mansion,' she said. 'That night, I lie awake and cried as I knew what my sister was going through with him. There was no love in his sex with us. On most occasions and before morning broke, he would bring us girls back to the shelter, bleeding and exhausted from our ordeal, before locking the chains onto our feet again. That was in case we tried to run away from here. But this night was so different for her. I knew Bulbul was not able to take it or somehow survive the ordeal. I could hear her struggles and screams through the stillness and darkness of the night.'

'Why didn't you help her or try rescue her from his house?'

Parveen had a crinkled face with tears streaming down from her eyes and replied, 'The Malik's son always placed us in shackles after we finished working all day. That was the last day I saw her alive. Bulbul had vanished, and nobody ever saw her again after that night. Sometimes I think I can hear Bulbul calling my name, or maybe I hear her cries in the wind.

'Back then, the other women and children who worked alongside in the pits set about spreading rumors throughout the brick-kiln workers community that the Malik's son had murdered her and had his men incinerated her body in one of the brick kilns just over there. I never go that side ever since as I can feel her presence there.'

'Mommy,' he said to Grandma, 'come here. Let's take a short break and pray for her.'

With this, the Christian ladies joined in the prayers that lasted more than an hour. after

***

Mommy said, 'Imran, Son, what are you doing over there?'

'I'm making a clay brick-kiln doll for my two sisters for Christmas. I'm going to bake it in the Malik's kiln if the master foreman lets me do it,' he replied.

'Okay.' She smiled in his direction while she continued to place wet soil into a mould on the ground in front of her.

Imran had carved a face onto the front of the doll's head in the image of a baby girl. He was etching the features with a sharp edge of a piece of glass. Carefully, he scratched the temple and crown with the family comb, giving it the effect of long, flowing hair.

'Hey, look, Mommy and Grandma! Is it okay?' Imran asked with an air of excitement in his voice but with his own rhetorical style.

'Oh! She's beautiful,' they both agreed.

Imran's grandma takes Imran by the hand over to the brick-kiln master and asked him to bake it.

'Okay,' he said. 'It should only take about two or three hours.' The brick-kiln master went on to say, 'Hey, Imran, you are very creative. And good work. I like it very much. It is beautiful. I am sure that your sisters will love it too when it is baked and glazed over.'

'Gee! Thank you, sir. I am very excited to see the finished article,' Imran replied.

'Did you construct this brick kiln, sir?' asked Imran.

'No.' The brick-kiln master laughed. 'This is a lot older than me. But many years ago, my grandfather, my father, and his friends built it for the old Malik—peace be upon his dead soul. The old Malik was the father of the current Malik.

'As far as I know, the design concept comes from the British Raj, Corps of Royal Engineers from the army. During their reign here in what was then India, they experimented with various types of kiln structures. The technology is not new as the Mongols and ancient inhabitants of this land were using fired bricks. And in places were plenty of water, suitable clay, and hot weather that they used to construct buildings in sun-baked bricks.'

The brick-kiln master said, 'The Bull pit trench kiln was designed by a British army engineer called Captain Bull way back in 1887. It's commonly known as Bull pit in Pakistan, India, and out across the rest of Asia. The Corp of Engineers had tried various shapes before settling with the elliptical layout. Look over there. See how the bricks are arranged into stacks with spaces in between.

'So the type of kiln bears the name of Bull pit after that gentleman then?' said Imran.

'Yes, that is correct. We owe him good respect for his engineering abilities.

'Yes!' Imran said. 'I would have loved to have lived during the time in India. My grandmas always tell me stories about them. Isn't that right, Grandma?'

'Yes, my child. I do like to tell stories about them.

'We have a lot to be thankful for to the British Raj. Did you know that the British also built the Grand Trunk Road? It runs all the way through Pakistan from the Afghan border to Karachi,' said the brick-kiln master.

The brick-kiln master pointed over to the stacks of bricks being loaded into the kiln for baking. 'Do you see how they place them? Well, that is to let the hot air pass through the gaps in between to bake the brick evenly and by distributing the hot air to reach all sides of the bricks. The hot air and smoke from the fire then enter into the portable chimney stack and depart as plumes of black sooty smoke into the atmosphere. Moreover, it is very dangerous as from time to time, some of the fire stokers fall into the kiln. It is a very hazardous job walking around on top to the stacks of bricks. Sometimes because of buckling of the stacks, some portions collapse, and the men fall inside. That's why we do not let anyone other than professionals up on top. Unskilled people mostly end up getting burned alive.'

'The Bull-pit portable steel chimney has been banned by the government because of the density of pollution and omissions. Why are you still using it then?' said Imran.

'I expect the Malik must be paying an official to keep quiet about it,' said the brick-kiln master. 'But let us not talk about that either.'

The brick-kiln master continued saying, 'We are lucky that they can't use the kilns in the monsoon months, mainly because there is no roof covering and the rains would pour inside then put the fires out. Another good thing to mention, we get a break away from bricks.'

Imran looked over to his grandma and said, 'But, Grandma, we still got to go to work in the farm fields.'

'Yes, Imran, that is right. But look at the advantages of working in the fields. We are given free bundles of fruits, sugar cane, and vegetables or whatever else is being shared out by the Malik for our efforts. At least, we get well fed.'

'Does he give us any money?' asked Imran.

'Of course not,' Parveen replied.

'Can I watch the doll as it gets baked in the kiln and wait with you here, sir?'

'Sorry, Son! I cannot let you stay because if the Malik saw you hanging around here, I would probably lose my job. But don't you worry. I will make sure the doll is baked to perfection, and I will even give it a bright, shiny, glazed finish. But only if that's okay with you.'

'Oh wow, yes, please, sir,' Imran replied.

'Anyway, then as soon as it is properly baked, I will call you over to collect it.'

Imran replied, 'Okay, sir.' He smiled and took hold of his grandma's hand, and they wandered back to catch up with the family still waiting at the bottom of the pit.

'Oh! Yummy! Great! Dinner is ready,' Imran said to his mother as she placed the brown-glazed clay pot of dal up onto a pile of bricks that formed a stable platform for the table.

'Fresh patties and spicy dal,' she said. 'Hey, Son, go fetch your grandma and sisters,' his mother instructed.

He called out, 'Come on, Grandma and good sisters, dinner is ready.'

'Don't worry, Imran. We are coming. We could smell it from way over there next to the dirt track.'

'What were you doing over there?' asked Imran.

'We were waiting to wave to the foreign tourists to go past on the old British army four-wheeled drive truck.'

'Oh yeah, but it's late today.'

'Maybe it's broken down out at the temple. I think that the driver will decide to stay the night as there will be too many bandits after dark.'

'But where will they sleep?'

'Most of the tourists that travel by truck are young and bring sleeping bags wherever they go. So I'm sure they will be okay,' Grandma said. 'Funny, but I just remembered how much I like my mother. Back there in Kamoke, she was always watching the travellers on the trains.'

As the sun sank low in the sky, shimmering, twinkling stars were already visible over on the horizon as twilight and dusk submerged the clear skies above.

A few hours passed before the brick-kiln master came by the front gate of Imran's house to personally deliver the tiny clay brick-kiln doll.

'Imran, where are you?'

Imran ran to the gate and said, 'Brick-kiln Master! Oh, mister, please hide the doll as I do not want to let my sisters see it before Christmas. Oh, she looks great. How can I repay you for the work you done?'

'Don't worry. I am only too happy to have helped you with your project. Have a good night.'

'Thank you, mister. You are so kind, and goodnight to you too. Safe home,' replied Imran.

With the dinner almost ready, the girls, his mother, and his grandma were busily preparing the plates and placing the food onto the table, too busy to notice that Imran sneaked into the house to hide the doll in his personal box at the end of his bed.

He thought, *That was a close call. If the brick-kiln master had come into the garden, everyone would have seen the doll. That would have spoiled the Christmas surprise for my sisters. Lucky, I was home too. Yes, it will be safe in here until we go to the celebrations for Christmas.*

The entire family, apart from his father, were sitting around the crudely built table, happily chatting and enjoying the traditional meal.

Imran said, 'It's a meal well deserved tonight as we all worked extremely hard today.' He raised his two hands out to give the food a blessing. All present bowed as he thanked Allah for the food. Imran watched in silence as his mother distributed the chapattis and spicy dal on each plate.

Neela said, 'Mother, make sure you keep plenty for father. He should be home soon.'

Imran started to eat his meal, at the same time excited, thinking of Christmas, and he found it very hard to try keeping the secret about the kiln doll from his sisters. He thought, *It's going to be great to see the enjoyment they will get when I finally give it to them for a Christmas present.*

With dinner finished, he hunched himself up on the pallet of bricks, with his legs folded up under his backside. Before long, with pleasant thoughts in his head about the doll, he had fallen fast asleep before his father approached the pit entrance.

'Evening, all,' he said on entry into the garden. 'Oh, you have had dinner already. Hope you managed to keep me some. Otherwise, I will have to go get some from the neighbor's house,' he said jokingly.

Grandma (Parveen) laughed in response and said, 'Stop joking, Mushtaq. Please come into the house. I will warm your dinner up for you. There is plenty for you in the pot.'

Quietly, Father picked the boy up in his arms and carried him home. Already, Mother had brought Caleb into his bed and was lying, cuddling the baby while humming a lullaby to help him fall asleep.

Suddenly, a cold wind began to blow, and the windows began to rattle. Out across the desert, all the signs of a sandstorm were about to come our way. Father said, 'I better go out and secure the camel and put a cloth over her eyes to protect her from the sand.'

He tucked Imran up into the bed beside his brother Caleb. That night, the violent sandstorm that lasted more than four hours thoroughly destroyed their old perimeter fence. They lost their family camel as they believed it got frightened with the force of the storm and she managed to break free from where it was tied up and ran off.

The winds had blown their garden boundary fence far away from their house, and by the time they got to the location where portions of it had settled, so too did many people from the surrounding villages. It was hard to distinguish as to whom the parts of fences belonged to. Everyone made a claim, and some fist-fighting broke out at the scene between the men and boy claimants as each person pulled and struggled to retrieve as much fence parts as possible.

Father and Imran came home with a few small sections of fencing. In fact, it was only suitable to fill a portion of the rear of the garden. Moreover, their garden soon suffered from erosion from the hot winds that gained access to the area. Their carefully planted and maintained garden of a variety of vegetables—such as tomatoes, potatoes, green string peas, and pot plants—were totally wiped out in one blow.

Grandma was very upset with losing almost all her crops. She sat on the old wooden chair in the courtyard, just staring out into space.

'This was a disaster. The camel was gone, and all our food crops gone too. No milk, and Father's livelihood gone in one night. What is going to become of us?' she said in a crying voice.

Mushtaq came to her side, placed his arm around her, and said, 'Mother, don't worry. We will be okay. It's only going to take time to recover from the harm the winds have brought. So let's get going and clean the house and gardens up. Then we will have some tea and go to work together.'

Father and his friends went in search for the camel but couldn't find any sign of her as the sand had covered up any footprint tracks that might lead them to where she was. The sandstorm left the terrain covered with a heavy coating of fine silted sand. All signs of human and animal activity faded away. An area where locals frequented to relieve themselves looked innocent enough as the storm hid excreted mounds unlike that of a well-concealed minefield.

Mushtaq returned later that night, and looking exhausted, he said, 'What are we going to do for milk now that the only source of it is gone?'

Asahi replied, 'We will survive, and God will help us.'

There was a sense of silence that night in and out of the hut as Daddy finished his prayers and leaned over from his bed to blow out the lantern while he whispered goodnight to the kids and their mother.

Imran didn't sleep, worrying where their camel could be. 'Hopefully, someone has found her, and maybe she is sleeping soundly with them.' But he began to wonder and thought, *Do camels have a heaven?* as he slowly faded into a light, uneasy sleep.

Within a short period, morning had come again, and before long, the household was buzzing as everyone prepared for another long day working in the pit. That is everyone except baby Caleb. Even so, Caleb still came along, strapped to Mom's back and slept on a swinging shawl that hung from the underside of the wooden charpoy bed. Occasionally, his grandma would attend to him to either feed or clean his bare bottom when he did his wee or his poo.

Two months had passed on since the disappearance of the family camel. One morning, Daddy had gone to Badin Town again in search of day labor as this was a task he had to do every day since their camel was lost—the only solution to replace the money he earned using the camel to deliver bricks to earn an extra income.

A burst of excitement filled the entire group.

'The pit!' Grandma shouted out. 'Imran, go quickly! I am sure that was our camel that just looked over the top edge of the pit.'

Imran, dressed only in his underwear, dashed off in the direction of her pointing finger.

'Wow!' he said to himself. He thought, *My father (Mushtaq) is going to be so happy, and we will have fresh camel milk again.*

The family camel stood proudly as she admired herself in the reflection of the still water while gulping it down from the narrow irrigation channel. This was the very spot where Imran's father and the children always used to bath.

The camel grunted and moaned. Plus, she appeared to be very happy to see Imran coming over to join her. Of course, she recognized him straight away. He was running, smiling, and cheering. The boy welcomed her back home. Imran knew that she loved having her neck rubbed, so he proceeded to rub her head and hug her neck. Imran permitted her to raise her head to swallow down a mouthful. He listened to the sound of it flowing down her throat.

'Okay, girl. Please have some more. You really must be thirsty. How were your adventures away for such a long time? Some water?' Imran studied her eyes as if she was going to tell him. 'Anyway, forget about that. You are home now. That's all that matters. Isn't that right?' said Imran.

'Oh, girl, we are very happy you found your way home to us,' Imran said with tears of joy streaking down from his muddy, tanned face. After the camel finished drinking water and had her fill, Imran said, 'Let's get you back to the family's front garden of the house, and I will tie you up to the new post that me and my father made for you.'

In the back of Imran's mind, he feared she would run away again after getting a taste of freedom to roam the wilderness of the desert. He wondered where she went and how she got food and water.

I expect she found water from the watering holes and maybe grazed on the wild grasses. But she looked so healthy enough anyway. She will be good enough to start work again tomorrow with my father. He continued thinking, *That was a good idea of my father to make the post to tie up the camel. And how did father know that she would come back someday?*

IMRAN'S CAMEL

Imran said to her, 'Down, girl. Get down, girl,' as she eased her front legs into a folded position before the rest of her body flipped down to become fully seated. As Imran clambered on board, sitting in just behind her neck, the camel gently swayed to and fro as she climbed up on her feet, standing so composed and elegantly, while Imran stroked and patted her time and time again on the side of her head. He told her of how sad he was when she went missing.

The camel seemed to remember the way down the hill to cross over the pit. Slowly, she maneuvered her way down the tiny track. It was a very slippery sloping embankment. On levelling out on the flat clay surfaced ground, she moaned and chewed her teeth, with saliva spilling on each side of her mouth as if to say, 'That was a dangerous task I've just completed.'

Grandma (Parveen) noticed too how she was also full of happiness. As she watched Imran and the camel made their gallant entrance into the centre of the pits, nobody hardly noticed the many bricks they had broken on the way across of the completed bricks. Imran approached full of emotion, with tears and laughter at the same time. He was overly excited.

On reaching his mother, sisters, and brother Caleb who had come forwards to greet the camel back home, there too were all the other pit workers, each taking turns to give her a pat and hug around the neck. Most of the workers had stopped work to catch a glimpse of the little drama unfold before their eyes. Small things and events such as this were very important to the community, and everyone joined in as one to enjoy the moment.

Imran, on arrival home, decided not to go back to work in the pits for the rest of the day. He instead spent the entire afternoon feeding and pampering the camel. He brushed the wild bits of thorn bushes from her light brown coat and carefully picked ticks from her underbelly.

He patiently watched the tiny gateway into the small courtyard of their house. He wanted to be the first to tell his father, just to see his face. He thought, *This will be the happiest moment of my life up to now. Nothing nicer had ever happened to me and the family. My dad is going to be very happy. Just think of it, we will have milk for baby Caleb and hmm… tea with fresh milk again.*

Mushtaq knew already that the camel was home again as, on his way, everyone from far and near the village whom he met on the way home had already told him about the camel finding her way home again. They said, 'It will be good to see you transporting bricks to the town. Don't forget to greet us and come join us for tea and a chat.' But for Imran's sake, he pretended not to know the camel was home again, and he looked very surprised when entering the compound.

'Oh look, Father,' said Imran. 'It's our camel. She has found her own way back to us.'

'How are you, Imran? We are so lucky as I did find any day-labor work in the town today. Now she's back, I can complete the back orders of deliveries of bricks to the town contractors. If you want and if mother permits it, you can come and help me load the camel saddlebags at the kiln.'

'Oh, Father, can I come with you and help with the deliveries to the town?' asked Imran.

'Sorry, Son, but you will have to help Mother and the rest of the family mould the bricks. We are way behind our quota for this month. The Malik was angry the other day and said he was going to put up the repayment bill again.'

'Oh, that fellow, I hate him. He only cares about his own pocket,' said Imran.

'Yes, that's right, Son,' Imran's father replied. 'But we are in up to our necks and have to pay him back for the house Grandma and her sister Bulbul built for us to live in.'

Referring back to the arrival home of the camel, Imran's father said, 'Oh wow, that is fantastic. I am very happy to see her home again. Let's have a celebration tonight. I have brought some mangoes, and we can share them with our family and neighbors.'

'Okay then, Dad. Let me help you load up the camel tomorrow morning.'

'Imran, you will have to be up earlier than normal as I will have to leave early in order to get three or four runs into the town. I can make good money and pay some to the Malik.'

'You will be very tired tomorrow night then,' said Imran.

'Oh yes, believe me, I am tired and hungry tonight too, and watching the camel eating is making me hungrier.'

Imran laughed while jumping up to give his father a hug. 'Great, Father. you are the best father in the whole wide world.'

'Gee, thank you, my son Imran. Let's keep her safe and secure,' he said to Imran. 'Hopefully, she never gets out again on her own. We have to thank Allah for answering our prayers.'

Both Imran and his father checked the rope to make sure it was secured tight enough but still comfortable around her neck and shoulders then rechecked the other end tied to the new post that they had built in her absence. She seemed to understand it was for her own good and stood there with a look of contentment while chewing on some straw. All of the family looked on, sitting under the small veranda on the floor.

'There, that should be good enough to hold her inside of our compound.'

'Gee! Father,' said Imran, 'I'm so happy to have our camel back home again.'

IMRAM WELCOMES HIS CAMEL HOME

Imran asked his sisters, 'Did you know that before our father and mother got married, their families came into an agreement that stated any boys born in our family would be raised as Muslim? As Mother is Christian, all the girls were baptized as Christian.'

'Oh yes!' said Sani and, in respect, went on by adding, 'Our father always was a Muslim. But I believe our mother was converted into Christianity. Prior, she was a Hindu within the traditional framework of society where she lived before moving here to the Sindh. Nothing changed when she converted as she is still classified as a sweeper—or worse, still an untouchable—and she will never be accepted into the mainstream of society and will always marginally live a deprived life.'

'Do you know who our grandfather was?' Imran asked Sani.

'No, I asked Grandma, and she just can't talk about him.'

His father didn't know everything, except he said that Grandmother (Parveen) told him that Grandfather had died a long time ago.

'Some kiln workers were talking about the Malik's wild life with the ladies before he was married. One laughed at me as I was walking past and said, "That's one of the Malik's little bastards there!" Everyone was laughing. So is the Malik our grandfather? What do you think did they mean?' Imran asked.

'Don't know,' said Sani.

'Maybe he is our grandfather,' said Imran.

'Don't you ever say that again, or I will have to tell Father (Mushtaq) on you,' said Sani.

'Okay, I will never say anything like that again,' said Imran.

Even so, the two were easy-going individuals who shared everything with equal respect and acted responsibly towards each other. This deal between the two families had upset many of the elders and mullahs alike. This further isolated them within the wider community, that is to say, with the exception of the Christian sector of the community. At Easter, Christmas, Muslim Ramadan, and 'Eid', all their family members shared the fasting periods of one another's religions in great, humble respect as they shared gifts together in a humble and peaceful manner.

On Christmas Eve, Thursday, 24 December 1987, the weather was colder than usual for that time of the year. The Thar Desert area and its semiarid to tropical desert climate for these months of November, through to February were the coldest ones.

Their extended family and several other Christian friends from their village tracked out away across the sandy desert. Their daddy was proudly up front with the elders, leading the way towards their destination, while Parveen and Asahi rode on the back of the camel. All the kids were comfortably strapped into a webbed rope–type bamboo that trailed along and tied to the camel's rear.

The journey was long but fun as everyone sang traditional songs. They clapped, laughed, and told jokes. That seemed to lighten up the boredom of the terrain and distance they had to go. Their group arrived safely to the mission compound as nightfall began, and their father, along with the other men, managed to get their tent up before they all went to join in on the festive celebrations.

Even though Father was a Muslim, it didn't matter; he was welcomed into the humble surrounds of the crowded Christian chapel of Matley Sindh. The group of people were already alive with the singing of Christmas carol. There were musicians playing a variety of instruments; the sitar, tabla drums, and harmonium are the main ones used in the Thar Desert. The smell of incense filled their nostrils.

Parveen looked around through a congregation of smiling bright teeth, the flashing lights, the candles. It seemed everything and everybody was decorated in brightly colored garments and ribbons. Such a warm and friendly atmosphere. Imran felt lucky to be alive and privileged to have such a mixture of family traditions.

The ceremony went on through the night, and all of Friday, 25 December 1987, Christmas Day, nobody seemed to go to bed. Even the children continued playing games. Imran awoke in the tented village that stretched out across the compound of the mission. He couldn't help but notice the sweetest smell of laddu (traditional sweet) being made by his mom in the corner of the tent. Imran, looking across at his father as he lay on his back with legs crossed, noticed his dad was singing a Christmas carol. How strange it was to him as he knew his father was a Muslim.

Imran said to him, 'Where has Grandma gone?'

'She is still praying in the chapel and singing carols with the other people there,' Mushtaq, his father, replied.

Imran asked, 'Is it okay, Dad, if I go to there too?'

Father stated to all present in the tent, 'Since our life in Thar is quite miserable and sometimes we feel starved for recreational activities, these types of gatherings and celebrations are a significant part of all our cultural lives, and it is important for the kids to mix with others within the community. I believe with him beside his grandma and sisters will make his little heart be full of pride and excitement. So let's provide him with that source of Christmas spirit and joy.'

'Oh yes!' his mommy, looking over at Imran, said in agreement. As Imran stood there, she said, 'I'm so proud of you, my son. Yes, your father is right. You can go to Grandma (Parveen) now and be with her and friends.'

'We will see you both soon! Bye then.'

'Oh here, Imran. Take some sweets to Grandma and your sisters. I'm sure she must be hungry by now,' Daddy said.

Imran outstretched his hand while his father poured in a handful of sweets. 'Please share them with the other children too. We have got plenty for us all.'

Imran excitingly ran off towards the chapel. Some people from the village arrived outside the family tent and called out, 'Hello, anyone home?'

Mushtaq answered yes as he stuck his head out of the open flaps in the darkness.

'Oh, hi there. Please come in. Season's greetings to you and your family.'

'Thank you for that and lifelong friendship.' They drank tea and entered into a general conversation.

Meanwhile, an hour passed by before Grandma came back to the tent where Imran's mother and father were sitting, listening to the sermon from the overhead speakers. Grandma (Parveen) kicked off her shoes outside while raising the flaps to gain entry in to the tent, lowering her head as she went inside.

'Where is Imran?' Both Mother and Father said in unison.

'Why is he not here with you? I didn't see him since earlier,' Grandma said.

'No, he is not here. He went to the chapel as he wants to be with you, and we gave him some sweets to take to you,' Imran's father replied.

'I did not see him around either in the chapel or with his friends,' she replied. 'I met all his friends. They are in the chapel, and they were with their parents.'

Mushtaq then quickly jumped up from where he was comfortably seated on the family rug on the floor. On leaving, he started calling Imran's name out at the top of his voice. 'Imran, where are you? Imran, where are you?'

Like the movement of a pigeon, his head bobbed around then up and down as he continued to search in vain for his precious son Imran. Not before long, announcements screeched out over the loudspeakers. He asked the security guards and even a police officer at the main entrance of the compound. They said, 'There are too many kids with the same description as that of Imran, but we will keep an eye out for him.' The police officer called it in to the police station in town through his walkie-talkie radio. Mushtaq thanked him before continuing with his personal search for his son.

The entire community franticly joined in the search for the lost little boy. The night became colder as temperatures plummeted over the now sombre group. It became clear that the boy was nowhere to be found.

Nobody remembered seeing him. He vanished into thin air. Grandma, becoming ill and going into a trance, was not making any sense. It's because she thought her son, Imran's father, was blaming her on the disappearance of his boy.

'Oh no, Parveen!' he cried out loud. 'Please don't blame yourself. It's not anybody's fault but mine,' he said, hugging and holding her tightly in his arms, while his wife Asahi massaged her feet.

She suddenly sat up on the rug. 'I know who can find Imran!' the old woman said with a glint of hope and inspiration in her eyes.

'Who, Mother?' said Imran's grandfather.

'Your father,' the old woman said. On hearing this, he moved away from her and stood, looking down on her and the others around her.

'What are you talking about? He's dead for years and years,' he said.

There was an air of silence as she cried out, 'Oh no, Son. He's well and fit too.'

'Who is he then?' he asked with a strained, soft voice.

Parveen said in reply, 'Your father is the Malik—the Malik. I was afraid to tell you, but it's about time I was honest with you. I've been so ashamed to tell anyone up to now.'

Slowly, Mushtaq walked out of the tent, forgetting to put his shoes on his feet and straying off out into the surrounding sugar-cane fields and soon was out of sight from all the people.

He said to himself, 'My god, what did I do to deserve such a life? What am I going to do?' He fell to the ground, burst into tears, and lay there face down. One of his good friends from home came to him and tried to comfort him. He cried out, 'Please tell me I'm sleeping and only having a nightmare.'

'Come on, you will have to go on. You will have to find Imran, you sweet, sweet son! He needs you to be strong.' He helped him to his feet as they mumbled and slowly moved back to the mission compound. His wife and mother were standing, holding on to each other. He walked clear past them and entered the tent where the children were already asleep and lay down in between them and closely hugged them and cried himself to sleep.

With the Christmas celebrations ending as morning broke under a cloud cover sky, he rose from his bed and fed the camel in silence and stood there, petting her on the head before he noticed a bulge on her tummy.

'Oh, I think you are pregnant. Are you, girl?' he said to his camel.

Quietly, the family gathered up their belongings and proceeded to make their way out towards the open, sandy desert. Parveen watched Mushtaq from where she was walking along behind the camel. As he walked, escorting the camel and trailer behind him, his head lowered in sadness, still trying to convince himself that the information about the Malik being his father was a fact. The children seemed to sense it and whispered amongst themselves to share their thoughts as to where their brother might have gone. This made the journey back home dragging for everyone, especially Grandma, Mommy, and the children.

On arrival into the family home, Parveen, looking to the place Imran normally sat for meals near the window, wiped her eyes on the corner of her headscarf, began to cry, and said, 'Imran is dead and gone now. We're not going to have him back home ever. Maybe we should start to invite our friends and neighbors over soon or at least after the Muslim Sindh traditional mourning period. As it's our honor, that's going to be questioned.'

Imran's father stood up shaking and shouted back across the table at Parveen, 'Stop it! Imran is not dead. He's just lost, and the missionaries and the priest said God and all the catholic angels are out looking for him and they will guide him home safely to us. So stop the nonsense talk and go to bed. I don't want to see you again today.'

Parveen slowly stood up, shaking still from her son's outburst, and said, 'Well, Son, I will be leaving too tomorrow as I'm a bad memory to you.'

He walked around to where she was standing beside the door and grabbed hold of her in both arms. 'Mommy, we love you, and I'm sorry about Imran, but you are not going anywhere today, tonight, or tomorrow. Never. Do you understand me?'

'Yes, Son,' she said.

'Now please settle down and stop blaming yourself for every little thing that goes wrong around here and go make some tea for us.'

Parveen noticed her son Mushtaq standing, staring in the direction of the Malik's house. She called out, 'Hey, Mushtaq, what you are looking at?'

He turned his head in her direction but said nothing in reply. She sensed his pain and started to walk over to him. He paused to take a puff from his cigarette and shouted out, 'Go away! Leave me alone!'

Parveen stopped and watched as he wandered off in the direction of the camel.

She thought, *Oh my god, what have I done?* then said out aloud, 'Oh, why did I tell him who his father was? Please don't let him approach the Malik. It's going to make things unbearable if he does.'

That evening, she tried to talk to Mushtaq, only to be told, 'Mother, stop it. I am not going to talk to him as he will probably throw us all of his land. Then what would we do?' Mushtaq held his two hands out and beckoned his mother to come have a hug. 'Now, Mother, stop worrying and go out for the kettle on the kiln.'

***

A few days later, Imran was awakened to the sounds of munching and hot breathing coming close up to his ear. Slowly, he opened his eyes, expecting to eye his mother teasing him as she would often do, but was confronted by the face of a buffalo chewing on straw that it was eating from the manger. As Imran became aware of his surroundings, he noticed that the animals' porcelain-like blue eyes by now were wide-opened in surprise with the sudden movements from the boy's thin body below.

As Imran screamed, the buffalo pulled back its head, causing the other buffaloes to scatter and jump around the stable. It's only then he realized he's not alone as during the night, he and three other boys had been put together in the manger by kidnappers. He tried to remember how he got there, rubbing his throbbing head.

It was the scariest monster-like animal he had ever encountered in his life up to now. In those days, buffaloes were not popular in the Thar Desert and were mainly found throughout the Punjab. Imran, up until now, never saw one there.

It was only then that it became apparent to Imran that his hands and feet were chained to the other three boys. As they huddled together, they sobbed and whimpered, crying out for their parents. But before long or even within seconds, the doors of the stable were opened wildly, filling the darkness with shimmering, bright daylight that created a spluttering thunder sound, followed by two scruffy bearded men running in, carrying rifles, who were extremely mad as they quickly approached the boys.

One of the men started to beat Imran with the butt of the AK-47 rifle, managing to fracture his already frail leg into two places, before the second man pushed him away. But he conceded after swiping and lashing out the rest of the tightly knitted bodies of the boys. Straight away, they proceeded to unlock the shackles of the other two boys and dragged them from the stable, leaving only two—including Imran—in the manger and still shackled to each other.

Imran cried for his parents through the excruciating pain in his right leg, sobbing and saying, 'Please let me go home!' as he was comforted by Tariq. In addition to his injury, he hadn't been fed for two days and had become very weak. He asked Tariq, 'Where are we? How did we get here? Who are these men?'

Tariq could not answer, shaking his head, really saying, 'I do not know.'

It's only there and then that Imran met with the boy who was going to be his soulmate and lifelong best friend.

The two men attended to the buffaloes. They opened the barn and let them out. Tariq watched with interest to see them heading away from the main building before making their way along the well-beaten track.

'What's happening?' Imran enquired.

'Don't know,' said Tariq.

After a long, boring day, sitting chained up, the sun began to sink lower in the sky. Looking out of the barn door, the boys noted that the buffaloes were returning. On arrival at the doors of the barn, the first ones in line hesitated. They just stood there, looking inside. But before long, they slowly entered one after the other. They were shortly followed by the two men. Carrying a bunch of keys, they approached them and unlocked their chains to allow them to do our poo outside.

Imran struggled to walk, holding his knee, walking alongside Tariq. They found a spot and quickly relieved themselves, wiping their behinds using handfuls of grass plucked from the verge of the foot track. One of the men brought a bucket of water to them, saying, 'Quickly, boys, get washed and come eat.' The boys stripped off their clothing and poured water over each other's heads.

Imran finished bathing first and waited on Tariq and said, 'Do you think they are going to kill us or what?'

Tariq replied, 'I don't think so. Why would they feed us then?'

'You are probably right,' said Imran.

Just then, the kindest man, the one who had stopped the other from beating them the first time, called out to them, 'Come on, you two. Your food's getting cold.' They nervously approached where they were sitting on a rug on the ground.

'Take off your shoes,' the man said, laughing out loud.

'What shoes?' the other man said.

They were pleasant to them and fed them well with chicken and potatoes with fresh water.

After dinner, one man said, 'It's time to go to bed, but tonight we are not going to chain you up. Look around you, boys. There's nowhere to go. There are big snakes everywhere, and the desert foxes will eat you up.'

'Don't worry, mister. We won't try and leave. Please, sir, can I ask you a question?' Tariq said.

'Okay, what do you want to know?' the man asked.

'What do you want from us? And where are the other two boys?'

'That is not any of your business. But do not worry. The other boys are safe and well and on their way to the camel races overseas,' the men replied.

Imran thought, *That's not true, or even if it is, it doesn't sound too bad a thing.*

Then trying to win favor with the men, Imran said, 'I can ride a camel. We have our own at home.'

'Okay that's enough talking. Off to bed with you two'

'Good night then, sirs,' both boys said then headed into the stable for the night.

As the boys climbed up into the manger, Imran said to Tariq, 'Do you know anything about the baby Jesus? The story of him in a manger?'

'No, Imran. I'm Muslim.'

'Yes, me too! But funny thing, I remembered it when I woke up in this stable and in this manger. I believed it must be a true storyline, and I would like to tell it to you.'

'No,' Tariq replied. 'I'm tired. Another time. Good night!'

'Okay then,' Imran said. As Tariq lay snoring in a deep sleep, Imran sang, 'Silent night, holy night, all is calm, all is bright,' before he too was fast asleep.

Tariq said he was eight years old. He said he came from Deri Ghazi Khan in rural Punjab.

'Myself,' Imran said, 'I think I was about seven and a half years old.'

He couldn't understand Tariq very much at first. He spoke with a different language and whatever he said came out with a nice accent. Imran noticed that his words were more like the sounds his grandma (Parveen) sounded like. But they cared for each other like brothers. They shared everything from hardships to happiness to occasional pieces of uneven bread to hugs and consoled each other after being beaten or being forced to work by their captors. But in hindsight, as they planned and schemed up ways to try escape, they found out the reality that they had not even begun to experience what pain was.

'Have you ever fired a gun?' Imran asked Tariq.

'No,' he replied. 'Have you?'

'No, so that's not an option until we learn how to shoot one.'

Both boys stood looking across at the two weapons lying on top of the table.

Monday, 4 January 1988

Imran's clay brick-kiln doll remained in his mother's (Asahi) possession since the day before Christmas Eve. She felt sad and wondered where he could be.

She said to herself, 'If only he could be here today.'

It was the biggest day for the girls as they prepared to head off to boarding school. She looked over to the picture of Jesus hanging on the wall of the sitting room as she went past into her bedroom, thinking about the good times they shared, and said to herself, 'It's a terrible tragedy not having a clue to whatever happened to him. How could nobody have seen him go out the gate? Or who? And if it were kidnappers, how did they manage to take him away without anyone noticing? I can't imagine he would have run away.'

She said to herself, 'I've lain awake for many a night, trying to find an answer to my many questions.'

She (Asahi) stood, holding on to the side of the bedpost, and glanced out the window and pondered for a while before being joined by his two elder sisters.

'Do you know he never got the chance to give you girls the beautiful present he made with his tiny hands?' she said. 'As he himself had never managed to hand it over to you girls back there on Christmas Day. I'm sure he'd still want me to give it to you.'

She carefully removed Imran's clay brick-kiln doll from the family heirloom chest located at the end of her bed. She unwrapped it from the cotton embroidered clothed, and the girls studied every fine detail that their brother had etched on the thinly shade figure.

Mother said, 'I can still remember the day Imran made it for you in the pit and the day of his disappearance from the mission compound. He strictly instructed both Grandma and me not to tell you as it was to be his surprise for you both. I was holding on to Imran's clay brick kiln doll, awaiting his return for him to present it to you in person. But today is a very special day. I think it's a good opportunity for me to present it to you girls on Imran's behalf, and I want you to promise to share and pray for Imran's return home and to remember your family and home while you are away at school with the holy nuns.'

Imran's sisters too were missing him so much. They cried, holding on to each other, as Mother passed it over to them.

Asahi felt the presence of Imran's spirit and his love and affection for his sisters. The two missionary nuns arrived to take the girls away to the boarding school in the Punjab.

Neela sighed. 'Of all the gifts we have ever received from friends and family like new clothing, new shoes, books, pens, and pencils,' she said, 'our most priceless gift ever is Imran's clay brick-kiln doll—the little statuette he had sculptured with his talented hands.'

That Sunday morning, the eldest sister (Neela) carefully packed it into the small haversack. Under the supervision of the younger one, she said, 'Be careful. Don't break it and let me do it.'

She gently placed it inside a cotton and packed some yellow straw around it to protect it from breaking along the journey.

Many of the villagers, young and old, had turned to bid farewell to the girls. For the occasion, the neighbors had cooked up a large pot of rice and spicy ladyfingers. Everyone was invited to join in and dished up a plate. The nuns had brought a box of traditional sweets, and the little girls, charmingly smiling, passed the sweets around to the elders and other children present.

One of the nuns said, 'Come on now, girls. It's time to go.'

They were assisted by their father who helped them climb up onto the seats of the cart while the horse champed at the bit in its mouth, adjusting itself four feet in order to bear the load. Next, the two Christian nuns managed to clamber on board too. Parting was so hard for the girls, but they shouted, 'Bye, bye!' and vigorously waved their hands at the locals. They headed down the dusty track. Before long, they were out of sight.

Mushtaq hugged Asahi while holding young Caleb up in his arms. They all stood and watched in silence in the same direction to view the car as it disappeared over the last sand dunes. Parveen stood, holding on to the veranda support post, chewing on a piece of sugar cane.

She said, 'The house will be even quieter now with the three children away.'

Mushtaq looked at her. Parveen soon got the message.

Then she said, 'Do you want me to make some tea? I'll go put the kettle on the kiln.'

He smiled in her direction and said, 'Yes, Mother. That would be very nice.'

A few hours had gone, and the girls and nuns had arrived in Hyderabad railway station. They were assigned a sleeper carriage to Lahore. They reached the Punjab after a long journey of approximately twenty-one hours. With the excitement, none of the two got any sleep.

The nuns said, 'Look, girls. We have finally arrived.'

As they entered the gates of the mission, they received a heartfelt welcoming from the waiting contingent of nuns and a large gathering of Christian girls—all residents who resided at the girls' boarding school.

On their first night, the nuns permitted the two sisters to sleep together in the same dormitory. Next day, according to age and class level, they were separated into two dormitories.

Sani felt very concerned for Neela. She said, 'Take Imran's gift to sleep with,' before she handed the clay brick-kiln doll over to Neela.

'Keep it close to your heart and cuddle it up overnight,' said Sani.

Neela was fretting for her mother and father. She already was missing her home in Sindh. She whispered to Sani as to not let the sisters know, 'I want to go home.'

Sani replied, 'Don't worry. We are safe here, and the sisters will look after us. This is a great opportunity to get a good education.'

She was finding it tough to accept her new environment.

On the second night, Sani could hear Neela's sobs echo down the hallway through the open doors.

'Oh, Sani,' said to herself. 'I better go console her before she wakes up the entire dormitory.'

Sani, to navigate her way to her dormitory, used the light of the full moon shining through the large collider windows to her advantage. On entry to the room, it was not hard to find which bed Neela was in because she was sobbing louder now.

Sani could find her younger sister Neela's bed.

On approach, Sani said, 'Come here, my dear sister.' Sani gently pulled back the blanket and crept in beside Neela to assist her get to sleep.

'I see you are hugging the clay brick-kiln doll,' said Sani.

'Yes, I am. Oh, Sani,' said Neela. 'I am so sad here. I want to leave here and go home to our parents. I don't like it here. Please take me home, please. Do you think our father sent us here for good? Does he not want us at home?

'No,' said Sani. 'We are here only to learn. We will be going home mid-break, and when we get there, it will be time for the camel to have her baby.'

'Really?' said Neela.

'Yes, it's true. The camel will be having the baby then,' said Sani.

Soon they were joined by the night sister. She softly said, 'Girls, what is going on here? Can't you two young ladies sleep? Don't worry, this is all new to you, and you will soon get used to us, especially when you begin to make new friends. Have you made any new friends yet?'

'No, Sister. Not yet,' said Sani.

'There are a few other girls from Sindh here too,' said the sister. 'I will introduce you to them tomorrow.'

'Thank you, Sister,' said Neela and Sani. 'That will be very nice.'

Sani said while holding on to her sister Neela, 'We want to go home. We don't want to stay here.'

Neela shouted, 'No, it's me who wants to go! Sani is just trying to save me from you beating me.'

The night sister (the nun) said, 'Now come on. Nobody is going to beat you, my darlings. Let's all go to the kitchen and drink some warm milk. I was just on my way to have one.'

They moved through the hallways and down the stairs under the guidance of the night sister (nun) and her small battery torch. Before long, they entered the kitchen.

'Sit up at the table, and I will warm the milk in a flash,' she said.

As the sister (nun) took a ladle-scoop full of milk from the large galvanized yern and poured it into a saucepan and struck up a match under the pan, a flash of blue flame ignited under the pan. The sister (nun) stood beside the stove in case it boiled over.

She asked the girls, 'Please, I couldn't but overhear you talking about your family camel. Is it true she is going to have a calf? Here, drink this warm milk. It will help you sleep.' She placed three mugs onto the table.

'One each. Enjoy this as Mother Superior tries not to encourage us to do this. In fact, she would be upset if she knows she missed out. Hehe!' The jolly sister laughed, and so the girls giggled too.

'Oh yes!' Sani jumped in quickly to speak. 'The camel will have her baby around the same time we have the term break for the summer months.'

'Great! You two girls have something fantastic to look forwards for,' said the sister (nun). 'And may I tell you also, your father loves you both as it was him whom we had to convince him that it was safe for you to come to school here. Really, Neela and Sani, stop worrying. Everyone here are very nice. Another thing, I am from Hyderabad. I am going home to be with my family same time, so I will ask Mother-Superior if I can take you that far. If so we can organize for your father or relatives to come there to the railway station and to collect you and take you the rest of the way home.'

With this, the two girls ran around the table to hug the sister (nun).

All three finished off drinking the warm milk, and the sister (nun) said, 'Okay, it's almost eleven o'clock now. Off to bed you go,' as she stretched out her hands so the girls were guided back to their dormitories.

Both girls went back to their own beds in the assigned dormitory and rested peacefully.

Back home in Sindh…

'Our home is very quiet now with Imran and the girls away. Only little Caleb running around,' said Asahi.

'You are very right. How I miss the children. Remember how I used to complain and count them on my fingers when they entered our lives. I would give up my life today just to have them all around me today,' said Mushtaq.

Asahi responded by saying, 'Well, come here, my dearest husband,' as she outstretched her hands. 'Soon, my dear,' she said as they embraced each other in the middle of the tiny room.

Parveen sat quietly on the family rug before saying, 'It is like the cycle of life all over. I and my Bulbul were taken here to Sindh from the Punjab, and now my two granddaughters are travelling back to the Punjab.'

They all laughed briefly before moving on to regular chores around the house and garden.

'It's time for our evening prayers,' responded the call over loudspeakers coming from the village mosque.

'It's our call to prayer,' Mushtaq said. 'Come here, Caleb. Let's pray. Face this way, Son, as Mecca is in that direction.'

As he began to teach the little boy how to perform the ritual, Parveen and Asahi fell on their knees with rosary beads in hands, facing a picture of blessed Jesus Christ on the mud wall and recited a few decades of the Christian rosary.

What a difference of beliefs, Mushtaq thought as he glanced over to the two women on the opposite side of the room. He thought, *Ah well, we all believe in one god, and whatever road we take in our lives, our destiny will join us together in death.*

He whispered to his little son that after praying, they would settle in to get ready for bed.

'Oh yes,' Daddy said. 'Good news, our camel is pregnant. I expect it must have happened after that storm when she ran away from home.'

'Oh! But that's not going to be good for you,' said Parveen, 'as a camel takes about thirteen to fifteen months of pregnancy to have a calf.'

'They can't run or carry heavy items on their backs either,' Asahi replied.

'So, Mushtaq, you must find other activities to earn money, which is going to be hard.'

'But we can still make some money by selling the calf,' said Mushtaq.

'Oh no, please don't do that,' cried Asahi.

Mushtaq shouted, 'Come on! Go to sleep. We will discuss it again tomorrow and find a positive solution. Life is full of surprises, sadness, but then God is great. Goodnight all.'

Meanwhile, back at the hideout…

Imran and Tariq found themselves that these guys were not too bad.

As things began to ease off and quieten down around, the boys began to get very familiar with the fat man. He was the one who stood up for them against the bearded, skinny one. So whenever the skinny fellow went away for supplies, he'd be gone for days. They never called each other by their names. He was playful and loved a game of cricket and brought them a bat and ball. With Imran's leg still hurting, they would leave him to bat.

With sweat dripping from the fat man's armpits and strong odor filled their noses, he ran past, shouting, 'Good ball! It's Pakistan, five runs, India zero!' in a childish sort of way.

But soon as the other one could be seen on the horizon, it was back to usual. He would wink at them two and say to impress his friend, 'Get that work done now, or you wouldn't like me when I get angry!'

Imran's leg was never right again his captors had just strapped it up roughly and never got proper medical attention. Leaving the leg severely damaged so much so, he lost a lot of strength in it. To ease the pain, Imran walked barefooted, clutching unto his knee with his right hand.

The two men said, 'Look, you two, we must go away together for a few days. But don't worry, we will bring back some good food, and remember, don't try to escape. We have eyes everywhere!'

Tariq said, 'Don't worry, mister. We won't.'

The area looked cooler and silent than usual. As Imran glanced out through the narrow slit in the door, he looked out over the horizon. The shimmering, slanting sun gave off an illusion of a caravan of people coming our way. (Was this an illusion or something else?)

Imran watched in excitement. Hopefully, someone or something was coming to rescue them and his friend Tariq.

Imran called out, 'Hey, Tariq, look! We are safe! We can go home now!'

But as they approached to the outside of the hut, they noticed the main man was the one who had beaten them. In silence, they looked at each other, with backs against the mud-splattered wall as they slowly slid in slow motion, lowering onto the dirt- and mud-covered ground.

As the days passed by, both Tariq and Imran were given chores around the farmyard, and Imran's favorite task every day was to go to the waterhole, escorting the buffaloes as more and more, he became familiar with the animals. As he played and splashed around in the swell, Imran even picked up sufficient courage to begin climbing up onto their backs while they waddled around in the pond. Imran loved to watch them close their eyes while he scrubbed and massaged their backs.

'Hey, Tariq, do you know about our rainwater catchment ponds in Sindh Province?' Imran asked.

'No, I don't,' Tariq replied.

'Water levels in these ponds remain at maximum level for six or seven months, even longer. There are many smaller ponds that become dry in less than two months. My father tells me about a mighty big river called the Indus. It flows from top of Pakistan to the bottom. But he said before it even reaches Pakistan, it is joined up by another one called the Kabul River. That river flows all the way through the mountains inside of Afghanistan. Then another four smaller rivers join up.

'With all that water and the monsoon rains, my father gets very worried, mainly because as the region where we are living is on lower ground and probably going to get flooded someday soon. At night, he makes our entire family pray for our safety. He explained to us in many a story about the great floods that accrued thousands of years ago when the Thar Desert was an ocean. However, a huge earthquake caused land to rise enough to block out the seawater from entering, and it became the dry arid desert it is today.

'My father also told me he'll take me to the barrage at Sukkur to watch the Indus River pass under the flood-control gates there. He and Grandma know all about water in Pakistan. They call it the hydrological cycle of water. At night-time, to pass the hours away before bed, Father would take out his old photo collection and talk about them. So many times, we must listen to the same stuff over and over. But we never get tired as he said we should know about our country.'

Tariq said, 'That's very interesting, but let me tell you a bit about the Punjab, my part of this wonderful country of ours. For starters, it's mainly a very flat land, and the fertile plains are irrigated by five enormous rivers. The Punjab means "five rivers". If you break the word in two parts, *punji* means "five", and *ab* means "water".

'During the rainy seasons called monsoon, our people witness an annual flooding period. With the general terrain being flat, the only safe areas in such circumstances along the rivers are the natural elevated grounds that are formed by silt that is push down from the Hindi-Kush mountains to become part of the Punjab landscape.'

Tariq viewed Imran as a very strange, enchanted, shy person; with some sad eyes, he carried a very wise head on his shoulders. He spoke of his father as if he were the king of kings, and the greatest thing he'd ever learnt was to respect and be respected in return.

Imran said to Tariq, 'You know, at first, I didn't know the way down to the pond, but wisely, I just followed the buffaloes all the way there.'

Tariq laughed out loud. 'I am from the Punjab. I know the behavior of the buffaloes. My father had about twenty of these type of domesticated water buffaloes on our farm. They are clever animals and work like clockwork. They know that when they are finished wallowing in the murky waters of the waterhole, it's time for bed. And they would steadily climb up onto the reed-covered embankment to head back home.

My father shared lots of fantastic stories about the buffaloes. He said the water buffaloes originated from India approximately five thousand years ago.

'Wow, that's a long time,' said Imran.

There are more breeds spread out across North America, the native Indians hunted them for many reasons, such as; food, clothes and they sowed the hides together for to make tents etc.

'Yes, and the buffaloes are used to till the land for dairy cattle and meat. They are a rich source of proteins and minerals. There is another breed called the swamp buffaloes. They can be found mainly in China and existed there since four thousand years, used as domestic animals,' said Tariq. 'Before that period, they were many feral breeds roaming around in the wild, and there are other wild herds across the Asian continent.'

Imran watched the buffaloes. At first, he was afraid they might decide to go the wrong way home and get lost. If that happens, he would probably get a beating from his captures.

Tariq laughed to see how Imran jumped about in front of them to get them to head in the right direction back to the stable.

'Don't worry, they will not run away. They are used to living here and know the way around. They have a great sense of smell too,' said Tariq.

'Hey, Imran, they are not silly animals, you know. And they remember where they live. Just watch and follow behind from a distance.'

Imran stood at the side of the embankment and was amazingly surprised as they all wandered alongside and into the stable.

'See, I told you,' Tariq stated with confidence.

'Yes, I'm learning. They are very clever and powerful animals,' said Imran.

Next morning, the men began to teach the boys everything they knew about camels from birth to death. Every day, for approximately two months, they explained with the aid of photographs and text in Urdu.

'There are two main breeds being raced where you boys are going. First one is the Omani breed. It has a very light color like this one in the photo.' He passed around the first photo.

'The Sudan breed are more of a darker tan color as you can see in the second photograph. Traditionally, racing camels are fed on dates, honey, milk, and a variety of seeds. The day before a race, the camels are not allowed to drink water and are prevented from feeding for the remaining twelve hours. With these two types of camels, the jockeys sit on a saddle behind the hump. So I want you to watch what you eat and start running every morning before sunrise in the cool of the day. It's important to keep listening and learning as our clients want intelligent ridership.'

The teaching continued for another few weeks.

'This lesson is to inform you of how the thoroughbred racing camels are, and we'll explain in detail how they are at first put through their paces. When they are about one or two years old, the animals are already able to obey basic instructions issued by the rider.

'To qualify at this age, the young animals must run a two-kilometre lap and in full gallop. It's then that the trainers and owners decide if it is financially viable and worth the effort to continue with training the camel for racing purposes. From then on, the capacity and stamina of the camels are increasingly lengthened by encouraging them to run accumulated distances every day. The distances are in proportion to the age and current fitness of the individual animal in question. Pay attention, you two boys,' the instructor went on with the camel training lessons.

'The camel meat and, in fact, milk are known to be very high in protein, vitamins, and other nutrients, providing an essential place in the diet of many nomadic people out across the Arabian, Asian, Chinese, Mongolian countries. It is said that the blood of a camel has very high concentrations of vitamin D, iron, salts, and minerals. But Muslim clerics forbid us to either use the blood or eat the meat.'

'Sir!' Imran raised his hand and said, 'Sorry to interrupt you. My family in Sindh province have a camel, and we only drink the milk. My father also said it's not good to eat the meat from a camel. It is harem (forbidden in Islam).'

'Oh, that's nice,' said the instructor. 'That is right, but there are special concessions for desert nomadic people. When there is nothing else to eat, they are permitted to eat the meat from the camel.

So, if you are tempted to eat the meat of a camel and the Arabs see you or find out, they will cast you out as they say a person who eats it is classified as unclean.'

'Sorry, sir, last question, please, sir. Have you ever eaten camel meat?' queried Tariq.

'Oh yes, many times, but then I am not a good Muslim. Am I now?' replied the instructor, much to the disgust of the other captor and the two boys who, by now, were making faces and pretending to throw up.

'Stop it now and concentrate on the subject at hand,' said the instructor. 'So please don't interrupt me again.'

'It's important that you learn as much from us here before you go away overseas, reason being if you are the good jockeys and win races, the Arab owners of the camel that you are riding on will reward you handsomely with gifts and money. They will hold you in high esteem. On the other hand, if you are losing races or falling off your camel, they can become very angry as they are bad losers. God knows what they will do to you. I have heard that they might just drive you way out into the desert and leave you there to die.'

The two boys, on hearing this information, decided to pay close attention to the instructor and didn't bother to interrupt the lessons ever again.

'In some cases, there is a wildly eccentric flavor to desert camel racing, which makes it a particularly entertaining sport to watch. It's not commonplace for camels to race for tourism.

Only it's a private affair but a memorable sight to witness a herd of camels and riders whipping away as they clumsily steam off at top speed across the open desert while heading off towards the finishing demarcated posts.'

'You know everything about camels,' Tariq said to the two men.

'Yes, we two were camel boy riders when we were young like you boys. We learnt the hard way, not in a classroom setting as we did for you. Someday, you'll want to repay us for it.'

Both Tariq and Imran looked into each other's eyes and, grinning and smiling, walked away.

'Why are we going to Arabic countries?' Imran asked the two men.

'They want young kids to race their camels in the Emirates because their own kids are too fat and lazy bastards. You will see very soon what we mean. Also, remember not to go talking to the police over there in the UAE as the camel races are non-Islamic, and it is a very controversial subject, not only in the Western countries but also in many Arabian countries too. Arabs tend to shy away when asked questions about what's involved and the gambling aspect.'

The subject could be quickly changed as per one incidence, an Arab was over-heard saying, 'Look at the photographs again. See how brilliant they look. Check out the beauty of these magnificent beasts. Look at them cruising along at top speed, with dust flying up off their feet that appear to rise, with all fours off the ground at the same time. They even give the appearance off gliding on thin air as they gallop along towards the finish post.'

The boys journey to AUE…

The first stage of the journey started next morning when they were taken in an old Bedford truck. Even though they were enjoying the company of a new person in their life, the truck driver chained them up again. But travelling on the rooftop over the driver's cabin by road, at least they could see the country. Tariq was a hive of information to Imran, showing off his skill with understanding the names of places on signboards along the way.

Imran asked him, 'Where did you learn to read?'

Tariq replied, 'I was going to school in Deri Ghazi Khan before I was kidnapped by these fellows. Oh look!' he said, 'That way is to Hyderabad, and that way is the Karachi. Looks like we are going to Baluchistan.'

Imran shouted back to Tariq, 'I don't know about any of them!'

'Karachi is a big city, population approximately eighteen million people,' said Tariq.

'Wow, how do they count all of them?' Imran enquired.

'They used machines and calculators, okay? In 1959, the site of Islamabad was chosen to replace Karachi as the capital of Pakistan.'

'Okay,' said Imran.

'But I think it happened in 1967. They had built a brand-new city beside Rawalpindi, and they called them the twin cities.'

Night fell as they arrived at a small fishing community on the coast, and the truck stopped just off the beach behind sand dunes.

'Do you boys want to get out and urinate before they arrived to get you?' said the driver.

'Okay, yes, mister!' they replied.

Both boys walked up on top and, for the first time in their short lives, saw such a marvellous thing like the Arabian Sea.

Tariq said, 'That's a lot of water, and the smell is so fresh!'

Imran agreed. They admired the bright red sun melting into it.

'How does the sea keep moving in and out?' Imran asked.

'Don't really know. We'll ask these men later,' Tariq replied.

As they maneuvered closer to get a better look, before long, a group of smelly old fishermen approached them from a boat anchored in the sandy beach and, at the same time, joined by the two original kidnappers.

'Well, these are the two boys you need to take out to international waters,' said their captors. 'We're going to pay your elders here as usual—and same number of rupees—when we confirm it's okay to do so and get radio message from the waiting smugglers, people trafficking trawler and crew that was waiting to take the boys to the AUE'

'Okay, let's do it.'

They walked towards a small skimpy fishing boat. It was rigged out with outboard motor attached to the back. It was very difficult to get into it, and Tariq and Imran were still in foot shackles.

One of their original captors opened the shackles and gave them a clap on the back, saying goodbye and good luck. 'Do your best work with the camel riding and show those Arabs how Pakistani boys can ride.'

'Bye,' we said.

'Hey, Imran, do you miss your family?' Tariq enquired.

No answer came from Imran's lips. Then he said, 'I am not sure. You know my father did not come to find me. Now look where I am going. I will never see them again.'

'What is the last thing you remember before you woke up with me in the captors' den?' Tariq enquired.

'I only remember my grandma at the Christmas ceremony at the church, telling me to eat some tablets. She said if I take the medicine, it will make me strong. As I swallowed down the tablets, I noticed two men were watching us closely, standing near to a car. I became very sleepy and asked, "Grandma, is it okay to go home to our tent?" She said it's better if I stay with her. I guess I fell asleep soon after that. Really, I don't know much after that. I do not know what happened or how I got to the captors' den. Only next I know, I am in the buffalo shed in the manger with you, Tariq.'

'So did your grandma sell you to the captors or what?'

For the first time, Imran was faced with the reality. He was trying to tell himself it didn't happen but, deeper down inside, believed that's what happened to him.

Imran pushed Tariq away and moved off to the front of the boat, crying, sobbing as he went, at the same time looking back towards Tariq, shouting out, 'I hate Tariq! I hate you! Go away and don't come back. Go now!' shouted Imran. The fishermen, sighted as they watch the drama unfold wondering what this was about. But didn't venture to ask.

Tariq moved closer towards Imran and outstretched his hand. By now, he too was crying, with tears flowing down his face. He said, 'You know, my father gave me away to the captors. He used the excuse that they were taking me away to be an apprentice mechanic in Karachi. I know it didn't seem right, but looking back, I could see he had not much choice. He had seven sons and three daughters to feed. These fellows forced me to swallow some medicine, and I too was surprised to wake up in the manger beside you.'

As the boat drifted out to deeper water, before long, the land was a distant image of shimmering lights from motor traffic moving along the coastal highway.

Waves lashed up the side of the tiny fishing vessel as its diesel engine spluttered and struggled to keep running while the boys sat closely together and watched as the shoreline disappeared from sight, with only an occasional flash eliminating the surface of the heaving waters.

'Do you have no lights to guide us to where we are going?' said Imran to one of the fishermen.

'Oh yes, we do. But if we turn them on, the navy will see them and come catch us. Then we will all go to jail. But don't you worry, we are used to this type of work, and we will get you to the ship that will take you boys away to UAE. We are using a compass and the bright stars above in the heavens to provide us with correct navigation and direction. We estimate it will only take us another five hours to reach the drop zone. So, you boys should get some sleep in the meantime.

'Okay.' The boys huddled up tight together and very soon were fast asleep. Tariq was the first to wake up and pushed on Imran's shoulder.

'Hey there, we have reached the ship.'

Imran rubbed his eyes. As the small fishing boat lined up parallel to the monster that rouse up high above them, they noticed some men waving from the top of the ship, shouting out, 'Come on! Climb up on board! Come on! Hurry!'

The fishermen shoved the boys' forwards to what seemed to be an entanglement of ropes swinging in and out from the side of the ship.

'Okay now, boys, let me tie this around your middle. Don't worry, you will not fall into the sea. I promise you it's safe.'

With shouts of 'heave-ho and up we go', the two little boys were swinging in and out and vanished out of sight of the small boat. Before long, both Imran and Tariq were on the ship's deck. Even though it was a warm night on the open seas, the boys shivered with fear, glancing down over the side. They noticed the silvery shadow of the swell as the fishermen's boat slipped away into the darkness.

'Welcome aboard,' said one of the sailors as he reached out his hand and continued to say, 'Let's get you inside and provide you boys with hot meal and warm bed. You still have a long way to go before you will have another meal and rest.'

The boy's arrival to AUE…

Early morning, the ship made its arrival known with a long blast from the ship's horn as if docked into the vast shipping port. The boys had to remain on the ship until late afternoon, reason being the customs official who was to provide them clearance was not working until then. In the meantime, the boys stayed below, watching the shipping containers being crane-lifted off the deck.

'I wonder how they are going to get us through all those customs and emigration people,' said Tariq.

'I have given up caring,' said Imran. 'I am so stressed out with my life. Really, I would love to be home in Sindh.'

'Oh stop,' said Tariq. 'This is a great adventure. If we are caught now, they will surely just let us go home to our villages and families.'

As they stood in conversation, a sailor approached, saying, 'Okay, boys, let's go. It's time.'

As they walked behind him. He instructed them to remain silent and said, 'Okay, here, a food parcel to help you stay strong along the rest of your journey.'

The boys thanked him as he pointed to the open door of a shipping container. 'Okay, boys, get in. I will have to lock the doors behind you. Sit on the floor as the crane will lift it off the ship and onto a truck below.'

The boys were lifted off the ground and quickly ushered into the open door of the shipping container. Inside were many faces with inquisitive eyes peering up at the, as they found a spot on the floor to sit.

Tariq said, 'As-salaam alaykum' (Muslim greeting) 'Peace be upon you'

And in chorus, the group—all boys in their own ages—said, 'Alaykumu s-salam' 'a typical response meaning' And peace be upon you too' followed by each boy shaking-hands with everyone present.

Before long and after a vehicle change, the boys arrived at the open desert plains and the organized settlement as the location for the camel races. By now, the boys were peering out of the camel trailer that they were transferred into somewhere along the way. All the group were mesmerized at the ever-changing sights unfolding in front of their eyes. They saw hundreds of Emirate Arabs, mostly dressed in white robes and traditional headdress; groups of suited expatriates; sophisticated diplomats; and groups of fancy-dressed women, with well-fed and, in most cases, overweight children.

'That must be those fat, little, overweight bastards,' Imran said to Tariq, and both boys laughed.

Everyone seemed to be enjoying themselves and the extravagance of the events. Others from a variety of consulates 'hurricane' around the betting stalls, chattering away, with US dollars and other currencies waving in their hands to place bets before commencement of the first races.

Imran quenched to think, *These wealthy individuals are worthy or even bothered to be concerned about the origins or welfare of us poor kid riders. Okay, we are well dressed in satin and silk clothing provided only that morning. Nobody cared that Tariq, I, and the other boys were stolen from our fathers. No one asked the reason why, we had to be duct-taped onto the skimpy leather saddle behind the camel hump. As the rest of the kids are fixed on top of their individual camel, groups of people gathered around, photographing our ever move. Others surveyed the crowd of onlookers. Tariq and I were scared as both of us silently observed the VIP gathering in the brightly colored stands dotted out along the start line.*

Tariq overheard a wealthy Arab who was more optimistic as he spoke to a smartly dressed, fancy foreign lady. He noted that he spoke with a hint of apology in his tone and said, 'Here in Kuwait, we take liberties and somehow acquire the usage of these young Pakistani children. Some people say it's illegal to do this. But we don't believe so as they get well rewarded by the camel owners when they performed well and win races for them.'

The lady asked, 'But aren't they a bit too young?'

'Ah well,' he went on to say, 'as with some as young as six or seven years old, not necessarily because they can ride or are good riders. But when they are strapped onto the saddle for the first time, they are so scared and scream so loud that it excites the camel into running faster, and the owner has a better chance of winning the race.'

He overheard another Pakistani kid tell how his friend raced the day before. But the strap on his saddle broke off, and he fell to the ground as the camels were running at top speed. As he hit the ground, the rest of the camels trampled right over him, with one camel falling directly on top of his back, leaving him in a pool of blood, only to be ran over by a few more camels coming from behind.

Imran watched the boy who was telling the story and said to himself, 'He looked familiar. Was he one of the other two boys taken away from the manger that day at the farm?'

As the boy finalized the story, he said, 'The boy died later that night, and they never brought him to a hospital. The other boys nursed him until he passed away in the camel stables.'

The camel bearers lined up the camels at the starting line. Imran looked over to Tariq. He smiled back in their direction and said, 'Good luck, boys.' Imran had never sat so far back on a camel before, so it took him a while to settle in sitting at the rear of the hump of the camel. But as being strapped on to the camel, he had no option but to do as he was told by the race organizers. The camels deemed to know that they were going to race and jump on one another's necks as they were standing close together.

The race marshal called out, 'Racers, are you ready?'

Some of the boys responded by shouting back in Arabic, 'Yes, sir, we are ready!'

The marshal shouted out, 'Get ready! Get set!' He squinted as he squeezed the trigger of the AK-47. Then he fired off a single shot into the air.

With lightning speed, the camels bolted off as the jockeys tensely held on tight to the skimpy saddles. The younger riders were screaming, crying, with the look of fear evident on their tiny faces, while the beastly animals galloped along underneath them violently, bouncing the kids up and down, in a trail of dust.

As we passed by the crowded and over packed VIP stands, people cheered so loud that made Imran's heart jump in his chest.

'Go, girl! Go!' he shouted out to his female camel. Imran looked back over his shoulder to see the whereabouts of his good friend Tariq, only to see the bright red tunic of his friend at the rear of the bunch. Imran's camel ran so fast that it was a few metres ahead of the rest of the field. The last and final stage, Imran could see the red ribbon hanging down on the winning posts as he came to the finish line in front, and alone, he crossed the line and won the race. Tariq's camel was not so lucky and came in last to pass the post, and he looked disappointed.

A group of smartly dressed men smiling and clapping Imran on the back spoke in multiple languages. The boy was confused, and with all the experience, he fainted and, as he was taken from the saddle, remained unconscious for some time.

A couple of hours passed when he finally woke up in a fancy bed and bedroom. He could hear voices coming from outside the closed door—a lady's and male's voice.

That language sounded familiar, he thought. *It's like Pakistani they are speaking.* He climbed out of bed to move closer to the door.

But as he approached, it opened, and the lady said, 'Hi, Imran. Are you feeling better as you fainted after winning the race and you were exhausted tired out?'

He replied, 'Yes, I feel good. Thank you very much!'

'Come meet my family,' she said.

The familiar aroma of spices cooking filled the air when he walked alongside her as she held on to his hand tightly. He couldn't believe it and admired the decorations and paintings hanging on the walls.

She spoke so softly and had good compassion in her voice. Imran studied her every feature as he had never seen such a painted doll. If these lips you venture to kiss, the color might all come away on your lips. But somehow they felt safe.

'And said where this place is, madam?'

'This is our family house, and this country is UAE, the United Arab Emirates. Hi, everyone. Imran is awake and wants to meet you all, and then we are going to eat dinner. Imran, this is my husband Muhammad. He owns the camel you won the race on.'

'Hello, sir,' said Imran.

'Hi, Imran, thank you for winning the race. You rode like a professional rider. I'm very thankful to you for that. These are my two sons, Ahmed and Rashid.'

'Hello,' he said as he shook their hands.

'Okay, later on, the boys can take you up to your room and give you your presents. Then you shower and change out of the racing clothes.'

Ahmed said, 'There are new clothes in your bedroom for you too.'

'Excuse me, sir,' Imran asked. 'Where is my brother Tariq?'

The room went temporary quiet as Muhammad whispered to his wife then said in reply, 'Is he really your brother?'

'Yes, Tariq is my brother,' Imran replied. 'I want to be where he is tonight, even if I should sleep with the camels. Is this a problem, sir?'

Muhammad replied, 'Let's see if it's possible. Go get ready for dinner first, and I will see what I can do to get Tariq here tonight.'

As they sat around the dinner table, Imran silently watched the other boys as they devoured down the breast of chicken by a handful. The mother requested him to eat up as the food was getting cold. Across into the corner of the room, there stood a wheelchair.

Muhammad noticed Imran looking at it.

'Do you know who owns it?' Imran replied.

Muhammad said, 'The chair belongs to Rashid. He can't walk since he was a baby. But he plays all sorts of sports sitting in it at school here in the UAE.'

'What happened to your leg, Imran?' asked Ahmad.

The house servants arrived in from the kitchen and started clearing away the food from the table. As Imran watched their every move, he replied, 'The bad men who kidnapped Tariq and myself beat me with the butt plate of a rifle.'

Again, Imran asked Muhammad, 'When is my brother Tariq coming here?'

'Don't worry, Imran. He's safe and probably asleep by now as it's late, and time for you and the boys to go to bed,' said Muhammad.

'Ahmad and Rashid, come on, get to bed, and take Imran up too.'

On hearing this, Imran began to sob and refused to move, crying out, 'I want to go home, and I want my brother Tariq.'

This upset everyone in the house, including the servants, and as they gathered around him, the mother began to beat on her husband Muhammad, saying, 'Go get his brother. How would you like it if your family were not here around you tonight?'

With this, Muhammad rushed over to the phone and, after a few minutes on the phone, came back with the news that Tariq was on the way. Imran was suspicious and really didn't believe them until the doorbell sounded, and within a short period, Tariq and Imran were reunited. Everyone was amused to watch the boys embrace each other, and they asked permission to go out into the garden to talk for a while. Muhammad granted them permission but then sent his driver and security gateman to spy on them for them not to run or try to escape from the compound.

The boys had never seen a real city and were bemused by the high shear of some of the skyscrapers within the vicinity of the wealthy suburbs of the city. They stood at the fence, peering out at the traffic lights, and counted how many times they changed from red, orange, and green again. The adventure they both had—exploring the vast gardens surrounding the mansion, the kelp fish swimming around under the waterfall within the pond—everything was new to them. But as they began to tire out, they spoke of the fun they had on the farm with the buffaloes and learning about the camels. They sat close and hugged each other on a swinging double garden seat, falling into a slumber land sleep in the heat of the night and under the watchful eyes of the family security detail.

The morning call to prayer sounded loudly from every angle, and the boys awoke, rubbing their eyes while watching the gardener and his laborers perform the prayer ritual on the front lawn. The birds were chirping in the trees. The fish were jumping to catch the floating mosquitoes on the top of the pond. Traffic pounded its way up and down the road outside the enclosed high boundary walls. Muhammad and the driver left, waving to them as they drove out the automatic front gates. They watch the gates close with sheer delight. The only communication with the local staff was done mainly by sign language and the odd greeting general Muslim greetings.

Next, there was a call out from the main doors into the house.

'Imran, Tariq, where are you? Breakfast is ready, come and get it. You boys must be very hungry,' the mother said. The boys agreed. 'Go wash your hands and freshen up before sitting at the table. Muhammad told me you boys didn't sleep in the house last night. Were you okay, out in the garden? Hope you didn't get bitten by the mosquitoes.'

'No, madam,' said Imran. 'We did not take the time to thank you for caring for us.'

'Where are your two sons Ahmad and Rashid?' asked Tariq.

'They have gone to school as it starts very early and finishes early afternoon, so you can play with them when they get home. Now eat as much as you want. You are in your auntie's house. So don't be shy. Nan and eggs with tea or lemonade.'

The boys ate plenty using only their bare hands.

'Muhammad called me a few minutes ago and said you boys will be racing today at another venue.'

'Imran smiled with excitement.'

But Tariq said he didn't want to race anymore and asked her if she could get him a job on a construction site as a laborer, even breaking rocks or helping with the gardeners here at the house.

She said, 'I am sure Muhammad will not be happy to hear that, so you better hurry up and get ready to go as the driver is coming to get you two and take you there.'

'Okay, then we will take a shower and get ready on time. In no time at all, they were washed and changed into their jockey-riding gear and waited outside beside the main entrance gate. This time, they were to travel in the family limousine to the racing track. They were excited to watch as the gates retracted once more to let the vehicle enter the driveway.

'Ready, boys?' the driver asked.

'Oh yes, we are ready,' replied the two boys.

As the driver opened the doors to let them into the front passenger's side door. 'You two are so small, both of you can sit in the front seat. Anyway, it's only a short distance today.'

'How far?' Tariq asked.

'Approximately one hundred fifty kilometres away into the desert. There is a strong wind forecast for that region. Only hope it doesn't affect the races as there are a lot of high-ups coming today from all over the world.' The driver had his music on and sang to every beat of the Arabic drums as they cruised along the open highways.

Tariq said, 'Now I know what it's like to be a tourist.'

On approaching the track, the boys observed the herd after herd of camels being led along the roadside.

'I wonder if any of those belong to Muhammad. He is very rich,' said Tariq.

The driver overheard the conversation and, in broken Urdu, said, 'Muhammad has sold all his camels and might be leaving back to Pakistan.'

Before finishing his statement, he told the boys he had not been paid by them in the last four months. 'There are some problems with cash flow in the family. Please don't say anything.'

The two boys looked worried as they stretched out their necks to see over the dashboard and out through the windscreen at the unfolding scene.

'Oh,' said the driver, 'that looks like Muhammad over there. Let's go that side and meet up with him.'

With a sway and a few speedier movements, they arrived right beside to where he was standing. He did not even turn to say hello but started by saying to the driver, 'Get the boys ready. They are in the first race. It starts in twenty minutes.'

'Okay, sir,' said the driver, and he continued to say, 'Come on, boys, smarten up now. You have races to win for the Malik Saab.'

The first race began, and Imran and the camel he was riding sprinted up to lead the pack.

Months passed by and day by day, the two boys, along with the driver, zigzagged out across the open deserts to participate in a variety of different races. Winning became a second nature, with both boys enjoying the excitement of becoming celebrities amongst the gambling camel community.

The daily routine passed—nine months of getting up at four in the morning, bathing for prayer, quickly swallowing down a little measured breakfast (quarter kilo of food in order not to gain weight before the races), and rushing off to the race course and back just in time for dinner and evening prayers on the back veranda to the sound of 100 loudspeakers chanting Muslim prayers and sermons before going to bed.

Back in the Thar Desert…

As promised, the sister (nun) brought the girls as far as Hyderabad by train from Lahore. Mushtaq had been contacted by the Catholic church in Sindh. He organized a taxi there and back to Hyderabad to the village. So the girls enjoyed chatting and finding out at the news.

Sani asked Mushtaq, 'Father, is Imran back yet?'

'No, I am sorry to tell you, not yet,' said Mushtaq.

All three sat and watched the road in silence as the taxi driver smoked a cigarette, blowing the smoke out through his open window.

The trip was long and finally they arrived home…

'Hey, Mother (Asahi)!' shouted Caleb. 'Father and Sani and Neela are coming across to our house. Quick! Open the door!' The boy continued to shout, 'Grannie (Parveen), come quick! Father's coming.'

'The entire community are coming too,' said Asahi.

'Let everyone come,' said Parveen. 'Let us all rejoice and praise the lord.' There was also excitement and happiness as Parveen announced the arrival of the traditional musicians from the surrounding sand dunes.

'Everything's falling into place,' said Mushtaq.

The camel who had reached her full pregnancy period was about to give birth. Caleb had grown and was very happy to have the company of his sisters at home again. All three jumped around and discussed what sex the baby calf would be. The girls wanted another female camel.

Caleb said, 'No, it's going to be a boy!'

Everyone laughed, and his father Mushtaq corrected him by saying, 'A male camel, not a boy camel.'

Many a villager had been patiently waiting with Imran's family there. Mushtaq marched up and down the garden, smoking many a cigarette, as if it were another child they were having. The girls had just arrived from Lahore on holidays. The village vet comforted the camel and stood with one leg raised on a chair, saying, 'This baby calf will be the thirteenth I've delivered this year.'

The wait last deep into the night. The girls had fallen asleep with the clay brick-kiln doll tucked up closely in between them on the charpoy bed. Parveen placed a blanket over them to keep them warm from the chilly desert wind. A clear sky overhead and the silver glow of the full moon gave off enough light over the onlookers. Then everything began to happen. The small tiny head was first to appear from its mother's body, and without difficulty, the rest of its body skippered out on to the straw bed.

'It's a boy!' someone shouted out from the group as a kind of joke after Caleb's comments earlier.

With all the noise and commotion, the two girls woke up in time to greet the arrival of their little camel. They both jumped up and gladly helped the vet wash the afterbirth from its body.

'Both mother and son are healthy,' said the old vet.

Everyone watched as the little fellow clambered to his feet and was assisted by the vet to find its mother's nipple to feed on. The musicians began to play traditional music on a variety of instruments—the sitar, drums—as the community celebrated in the normal sense of happiness.

'Oh, Mommy, Daddy, can we call him Imran after our brother Imran?'

'Okay, that's a good idea,' said Mushtaq.

With this the people started to drift off to their homes. Already, dawn was breaking, and birds were chirping and fluttering about to welcome the new day and the new baby camel. Many children stopped off to visit the house and spent fun times together with Caleb, the girls, and the baby calf. Every now and then, they looked back to the windowsill to where the clay brick-kiln doll stood proudly, overlooking the playing children and camels in the compound.

Across the ocean in the UAE...

Because of the international media's attention, the controversy into camel racing using children and their exploitation became known. The UAE police had started an investigation into illegal gambling and racketeering was well under way by local authorities. Ringleaders who were responsible for money laundering activities were arrested.

That included activities surrounding Muhammad's mansion. It surfaced when the family gardener could hear the screams of police sirens getting louder and louder. He managed to call Muhammad on his phone beforehand as five or six police vehicles came to a screeching halt outside the main gate. There were police officers in full swat-team gear who forced open the main gates into the compound, briskly bursting their way through the front hall door into the house. The gardener stood motionless with a set of grass-cutting spears held open within his both hands. The cook was marched out onto the front lawn to join the gardener. Both men stood trembling in their slip-on shoes as they could clearly watch through the sitting-room window. They could see the raiding party dismantle items of furniture.

'What are they looking for?' the cook asked the gardener.

'Must be drugs or money. I don't know.'

Perhaps, Muhammad must have known in advance that his house was about to be raided by the police. Did he get a tip off? Or was he just lucky that none of his family were at home when it happened that morning.

Muhammad was away at the camel racetrack, and the wife was already back in Pakistan. The police arrested all his staff and put a warrant out for the arrest of him and his wife. Did he get inside information in a timely manner for his wife and children to make plans to do a runner?

Luckily for both Imran and Tariq, Muhammad's two sons were at home in Pakistan on school holidays, staying with his wife's mother in Quetta.

Muhammad promptly joined the group of boy jockeys as they waited to mount up onto their respective camel. He turned to Imran and Tariq, saying, 'Go back to the driver fast and don't stop for anything. Wait there. I'll be coming soon too.'

Muhammad and the Pakistani family helped Imran and Tariq escape from the clutches of the camel-racing racket and paid fares on a ship bound for Pakistan.

The driver returned to the house and picked up a wheelchair and brought it to the shipyards where he had dropped off the boys and

Muhammad earlier. On arrival, there were a few other vehicles parked up at the shed. As he approached, the doors slid open and out popped Muhammad showing the boys he had a passport with his two sons' names.

The plan was he would be smuggling the boys by using his son's names. The wheelchair would be used by Imran. As nobody would suspect anything was wrong as his son also had problems walking like Imran did. Within a short time, a group of men arrived and joined up with Muhammad and his driver inside the shed. Shortly after, the driver came out with a bundle of money in his hand and a smile on his face. He said, 'Bye, bye,' and headed off out the gate, walking, leaving the vehicle behind him. Obviously, he received his salary with a bit more to keep him quiet as Muhammad made good his escape.

'What's going on?' said Tariq to Imran.

'I think he's taking us home to Pakistan.'

The two boys were nervous and watched with deep suspense as some men came and went again. Two hours or more had passed before a man came and called the boys and told them to follow him inside. They hesitated and looked at each other and said, 'What have we got to lose? Let's go in!'

Muhammad said, 'Stand over there with your backs against the wall. You're going to have your photos taken for the passports.'

As they stood there, Muhammad stated that good impersonations and character behavior was in order. 'If we're going to get this right, the immigration authorities in Pakistan are used to people smugglers and the tricks they play. Therefore, to pull this off successfully, we will need to teach you both how to become Ahmed and Rashid. Okay, boys?'

'Yes, sir.'

'Imran, because of your bad limping leg, we will put you into the wheel chair. And, Tariq, you can push him along. To do this, you both need to know how to fold and open the chair and do it without making mistakes. Imran, you must remember not to walk or you will draw the attention of the officials at the port. It will be okay to walk on board the ship. But whenever we get to Pakistan, stay in the chair.'

'Yes, sir. I will!'

'Now go around behind those containers and get changed into my son's clothes. They should fit you perfectly.'

Within a few minutes, the boys came back fidgety, looking awestruck in Western jeans, shoes, T-shirts, and jackets.

Muhammad laughed and said, 'Look at the two of you. I'm very impressed. Okay, we don't have much time, so let's go.'

Muhammad led the way outside to head down the entrance into the port. Security scanned their bodies, and without hinder, they were permitted entry and joined up with other passengers and crew waiting to get through emigration. Tariq and Imran played the part to a tee and, before long, were on board the ship.

This time, they were made comfortable below deck in a twin-berth cabin. They lay down on the beds while listening to the sound of the ship's horn. The gentle sway of the cabin indicated that they were finally going home. As both boys stood up again on the floor, they embraced arms around each other's shoulders. They exchanged ideas on what's it going to be like to be home again.

As groups of seagull scavengers were in flight soaring high above the ship's deck, some sailors were playing cards and drinking alcohol. Another few seagulls were flying around outside of the boys' cabin. They enjoyed watching them out through the circular window. The gulls flew about with their brilliantly shimmering white feathers flashing in the sunshine to a backdrop of pale blue sky and emerald-colored sea. How happy the boys were.

Muhammad knocked the door before entering the room. 'Okay, that show you put on back there for the emigration authorities was fantastic. You both did very well. Thank you.'

The boys smiled back as they viewed and smelt the plates of food that Muhammad was carefully carrying as not to drop it on the floor. 'Here is dhal, chapattis, and this is Pakistani cha made with milk and best quality Indian tea. I hope you enjoy it, and if you need any more food, just knock on my door. It's just next door on your left-hand side as you walk along the passageway.'

'Okay, sir, thank you very much for your kindness and hospitality.'

'Oh yes, you can go outside on the decks to get some fresh air in your lungs. But be careful and don't go near the sides as you could fall in the sea and become shark meat.'

'What's a shark?' Imran asks Tariq as they settled down to eat the meal.

'They are joint fish. There are thousands and thousands of them in the sea. My teacher showed us a picture of one back in Deri Ghazi Khan, very scary, and they grow bigger than this room in length,' said Tariq.

'Oh no, so you are telling me that there are lots of sharks swimming around our ship right now?' asked Imran.

'Oh yes! And they would love to eat you or me for dinner,' replied Tariq.

'Hey, Tariq, let us go outside and play a game!'

'Okay then.'

They looked out through the door. The air was crisp and fresh as they ran around on the upper deck and played a game of hide-and-seek in between the stacks of containers. They chased the seagulls and waved to a passing ship.

As darkness fell across the now-empty ocean and the cold winds began to blow, the boys went back to our cabin and went to bed. Later, they were woken up, rolling back and forth by a stormy sea. It was raining heavily as it lashed across the tiny round windows on the cabin wall.

'Tariq, can you see what I see?'

'Yes,' he replied. 'I see flashes of lightning, but it's far way off in the distance.'

As they stood by the window, Imran pointed to the large pale moon and the sparkling stars that peppered the now-darkened sky. As the wind howls through the tiny gaps of the door, suddenly, there was a loud bang and scraping sound that seemed to come from under the ship, followed by shouting and screaming along the passageway.

Before long, Muhammad peered in through the door, saying, 'Come on, boys! There's been an accident, and the ship is taking on water. We have been instructed to go on the upper deck for a possible evacuation into a lifeboat.'

Tariq and Imran hurriedly grabbed whatever belongings they could and held hands to follow Muhammad up the stairs.

By now, every passenger—numbering around sixteen or more—and crew alike were putting on life jackets.

Seems sad when life was starting to get better, Imran thought but bravely ensured Tariq that everything was going to be all right. They stood shivering while the captain decided if it was totally necessary to abandon the ship.

A decision was made to allow only the passenger to climb into the lifeboats as he ordered his crew to man a variety of positions and start to attend to trying to mend to the hole in the port side. The captain wished us a safe trip and said a mumbled prayer.

Through the mayhem and as the lifeboat was lowered into the sea, both Tariq and Imran wondered why he didn't let the crew and even himself escape in the boats. Before long, all the commotion had ended, and the ship faded off into the darkness and swollen ocean. There was silence now where before there were shouts of help, and the drone-like sound of the ship's foghorn was now only a distant memory that quickly disappeared as more personal drama unfolded in front of them.

The survivors sat motionless as they bobbled up and down while listening to the clattering of the lifeboat outboard motor, and huddled close together, the boys fell asleep. Time passed by, and the rain began to fall, and soon the boat filled up with water. Without warning, it capsized, throwing the twelve people out into the sea. It was difficult to find anyone in the darkness of the night.

Very soon, it was a fight for everyone to find something to hold on to. Luckily enough, some items of debris were floating around, so Muhammad passed a timber plank over to Imran to hold on to.

'It must be debris from the ship's furniture,' Muhammad said.

'Where's everybody gone?' said Imran. 'Where's my brother Tariq?' He called out to the open sea as it ignored him and trashed out with an unforgiving array of massive thirty- to forty-foot-high waves.

Imran believed he saw Tariq go down under the water. He called out to Muhammad to go rescue him, but he was nowhere to be found. Imran fretted for his lost brother, while everyone else was sure he had drowned and was to a watery grave like the others. They approached Imran and proceeded to hug him in their arms to console him.

'Your brother was a good boy, and Allah will take him straight into paradise. It's his will.'

This was no comfort to Imran as he tried to struggle free, shouting out, 'Why? Why did you take me only? Friend and brother… don't you know how much I need him with me? Why?'

Muhammad said, 'Please, Imran, I will care for you like my own sons.'

'I don't want to live with you! It's mostly your fault anyway! If you bastards didn't take us away from our families in the first place, none of this would have happened, and we'd be safe and well, living in our own homes. You bastard! Who do you think you are?'

Muhammad looked embarrassed, glancing around at the others. He still tried to convince Imran of his commitment to take him home. While squeezing Imran close to his chest, he too began to cry, saying, 'I'm sorry! I'm really sorry for your loss. I promise I'll do my very best to get you home to your family.'

'When? Then when can I be with my family?'

'I don't know,' said Muhammad.

What remained of the tiny lifeboat bobbed around in the water and struggled to stay upright and afloat in the stormy seas. The storm had gone now as the sun showed its face in the early morning rain. A scream drew the attention of the group of survivors in a land off in a distance. This encouraged them to start moving in the same direction. After a short while, they managed to climb up the rocky shore edge to the dry ground.

'Where are we?' Imran enquired. But nobody could reply.

Then someone said, 'I think it's Pakistan or maybe Iran.'

'Why would you say Iran?'

'Well, we were approximately three hours out of the gulf, and just before dark, I overheard one of the crew say we were near to the coast of Iran.'

'What time is it?' said Muhammad, holding his hand up to block the sun from his eyes.

Another man replied, 'Going on the sun, coming up in the eastern sky. It's about eleven o'clock. In approximately one hour from now, the shadow of the sun will be at its shortest point, and therefore, it will be twelve o'clock or noontime.'

'What are we going to do then?' Imran asked.

Muhammad said, 'Well, we will have to try find some food and water somewhere soon. This sun will get very hot also, so we are also going to need shape. But there's nothing around here. All four of us will need to stay together, and let's head out there. Surely, there must be some friendly people living here.'

Just then, Imran noticed a person floating in the sea.

'Hey, look out there! Someone from our ship, I think. Let's try see if he's alive.'

'Oh, it looks like Tariq,' Muhammad said. 'I'm the only one who can swim. I'll go get him.' With that, he jumped into the sea and, within a few minutes, managed to retrieve Tariq's limp body from the sea.

Muhammad pumped on his bare chest. Suddenly, Tariq spat up water and opened his eyes, much to the surprise of all four standing around him. Imran jumped around with joy and excitement and looked up to the heavens and shouted, 'Yeah, Allah be praised! Thank you! Oh, thank you!'

Muhammad stood there again on the barren shore, soaked to the core. He sighed and said while picking up a parcel he had been carrying close to his side ever since he left the UAE, 'Come on. Let's start moving away from the coastline before the navy coast guard finds us. They'll be out searching for our ship. I'm sure the captain would have called in an SOS. So this is our opportunity not to be discovered, or maybe we will end up in prison in this country. So until we are safe, let's work as one to survive.'

One of the other two men helped Tariq along and, at times, carried him up on his shoulders. By now, the group had been walking barefooted on the rough, rocky ground and under the hot, bright sun. The biggest difficulty was not having food or water. Muhammad looked back to where they had come and thought it didn't look like they had moved or gained a lot of ground. He started to become very aggressive towards the other two strangers and ordered them both to carry Tariq and Imran and to pick up the pace.

Another hour of hiking over the rough terrain when one of the men suddenly fell and said to Muhammad, 'Look over there! I think it is some sort of factory or settlement. Can you make out what country flag that is on the pole?'

'No, it's too far away for my eyes. Hey, Tariq, Imran, can you tell what colors are on that flag?'

'Oh yes, sir. It's green and some white also.'

'Great, we are in Pakistan. It must be Baluchistan as we can't possibly be far enough east for it to be Karachi port,' said Muhammad.

'Anyway, we better be careful, and I think we should wait until dark to go there in case it's another country all together.'

'Yes! I agree,' said the older of the two men.

As all five lay on the ground, wondering if it were Pakistan, a group of men approached from behind them. They came on camels and had been watching from far away.

One shouted out in a foreign language, 'Who are you? And why are you all watching the port like that?'

Slowly, Muhammad stood up with his hand above his head. He whispered for them not to move as they were all carrying weapons of some sort. 'I think they have AK-47s.'

'Okay, we'll stay on the ground,' said Tariq.

'Did you arrive here on a boat? And if so, which country did you board the ship?' enquired one of the men sitting on a camel and towering high above them.

'We arrived here from AUE and we think that ship we travelled on might have sank' replied Muhammad.

Muhammad moved forward to meet them with his hand stretched out to shake their hands before one of them said, 'Don't make a mistake, mister. We are not your friends.'

'Sorry,' said Muhammad and stopped dead in his tracks. 'We are Pakistanis—me and my two sons. I can prove it. I have our passports in here. Isn't that right, my sons?' As he reached down to take the passports out of the parcel, he continued to say, 'These two men are from…'

Before Muhammad could say where they were from, one of the camel riders fired off a burst of AK-47 rounds and shot both men dead on the spot as they both lay in a pool of blood.

The leader, an old man, called out, 'Come here, boys. We know he was not your father by the way you reacted to his instructions before we came over here.' He raised out him arms and said, 'Come here, my children, you are now free of this tyrant. Come here, boys, your ordeal is all over now.'

Both Tariq and Imran reluctantly and slowly went to his side before another rider shot Muhammad dead on the spot where he stood. The boys were so frightened, they both wet themselves as they stood embraced in the stranger's arms.

Shortly afterwards, Imran was sent over to search all three bodies and take whatever they were keeping in their pockets. Imran had never seen a dead person. He tightened up his belt on his jeans and slowly moved over to the first body.

'Yes, take everything to me,' the old warrior Afghan man said, 'especially that box from him.' He pointed towards the corpse of Muhammad. Imran quickly held one hand over his mouth in order not to get sick and picked up the box that Muhammad held so close all the way to his destiny.

'Now bring it here,' said the old Afghan warrior. 'Okay, good boy.'

With that, he pointed his rifle at Tariq's head and proceeded to pull the trigger but hesitated, saying, 'You boys are now my property and are coming to our encampment to live out your days in my services.'

'Oh thank you, mister. Please don't kill us. We will be your obedient servants. Your wish will be our command.'

At the same time, Imran thought, *Oh, where am I, and who are these men?*

As the group mounted up on their camels, the boys managed to whisper to each other. Tariq said, 'Look, there's about two hundred of them and all those camels and guns.'

'Who are they?' Imran wondered and shook his head.

Tariq noticed that one young boy his own age was smiling across and taking advantage of an opportunity to make a smile back before his father had noticed and shouted at him to ride on. As they travelled across the country, the old warrior passed drinking water over to the two boys. The camel train was escorted by a pack of extra-large dogs.

Tariq stated, 'I think these people are Kuchi nomads like people from Afghanistan. I saw photos of similar type tribesmen in school. Seemed like days not hours that passed by before we reach the encampment.'

Women and children ran to greet their respective fathers or sons returning home.

'Who are these two boys then?' asked the old man's wife.

We found them wandering in the desert sands. So they will now live with us, and they can help mind the sheep and goats with our boys. By the way, we killed their older friends.'

'Why?'

'I didn't like the way they looked at us. So I ordered Faridullah to shoot them dead. Anyway, my dearest wife, I've brought you a gift.'

Imran and Tariq watched in silence as the old lady broke open the tightly sealed parcel. They noticed their forged passports in the bundle, along with Muhammad's passport and a huge pile of US dollars.

'So that's why he didn't want to leave it out of his hands,' said Tariq to Imran.

THE KUCHI ENCAMPMENT NEAR AFGHANISTAN

The Kuchi community's encampment stretched out across the hills as far as the eye could see. The hills were dotted with campfires with black family tents and grazing goats and sheep. There were hundreds of camels, and children playing games were running here and there throughout the meadowlands. The old Afghan warrior called out to his young son, 'Hey, Arif, where are you? Come meet your new brothers welcome.'

Arif gripped onto his rifle and quickly placed it over his shoulder and ran over to his father's side. His father reached out to greet him as Arid bowed in a gesture of holiness and kissed his dad's two feet while his father placed his two hands on the boy's temple, saying, 'Bismillah Rahman Raheem and so on. Now, Arif, go take the boys and let them bath in the natural springs over the hillside.'

'Okay, Papa,' he replied.

All three boys headed up and over the hilltop. Arif was so happy to have new friends or, as his father mentioned, brothers. Tariq and Imran again whispered to each other, 'How are we going to escape from this lot?'

Neither had any ideas at this stage.

'Did you see where the old lady put our passports?' Imran laughed, and both blushed. 'Yeah, down the front of her clothes.'

They giggled and laughed.

'Okay, let's enjoy our bath.'

All three boys splashed and played around in the water until Asif's mother came to take them back. It was just before dark, and the aroma of goat meat filled the air.

'Hi, Asif. Who are you and your people?' We are Afghans, and because the Russians are occupying our country, my father moved our people over here to Baluchistan for safety.

But we still fight the Russians and support the struggle of our people. You will see something very special, and as you are my Muslim brothers, you'll probably offer to help our country too.'

Asif had one duty—to feed his father's camel. He invited Tariq and Imran along to watch. Tariq explained to Arif that he owned a camel in the Sindh Desert. He also told him of the experiences they had, such as camel racing in the UAE. The stories really impressed Arif so much, so he told his father and mother about them when they were having dinner.

Later that night, as they lay awake talking about Muhammad and his family, they felt a little bit sad that the boys had now lost their father. They spoke of how lucky a day today was.

'I think we will be okay with this community,' said Tariq.

'Do you think we will ever see our own families ever again?' enquired Imran.

'Of course, we will. Now as we grow from boys to men, let's make a blood pact together.'

Both boys cut each other's hands only just slightly to draw blood and shook hands, much to the amusement of Arif who laughed and laughed himself to sleep. Under a million stars shining from the heavens outback somewhere in Baluchistan, they fell fast asleep huddled up together with their new-found brother.

Next morning, the boys were taken by a Bedford truck to Pakistan's Gadani ship-breaking yard. They travelled for hours before reaching one of the world's largest ship graveyard operations.

The yard was located on a ten-kilometre stretch of beach at Gadani which was located approximately fifty kilometres northwest of Karachi. The old Afghan warrior explained that along this stretch of beach, ship dismantling and breaking had been taking place since before Pakistan's independence. Gadani district currently had an annual capacity of breaking over a hundred ships.

Business was booming since the seventies because of the increase in the price steel on the world market. Here, the steel from the ships was stripped systematically shortly after it arrived up on the shore.

'Can you see those factories out over there? They melt the steel into various sizes called billets and other facility's manufacturer reinforcement steel bars for the construction industry. In fact, this entire area is vital for the economy of Pakistan.'

'But why are we here, sir?' asked Tariq.

'Well, I think you will find work here, and I can make money by selling you two as laborers to the Malik.'

'Look over there,' said Imran. 'Is that the ship we were on with Muhammad?'

'Oh yes, that's it, all right. So it was not the storm that night, and it didn't sink after all.'

On hearing this, the old Afghan warrior began to laugh, saying, 'You should have stayed on board as they were only ten kilometres from here when your lot was ditched. The captain makes extra money each time he takes ships here to the ship graveyard. Mostly, his passengers are drowned when he decides to get rid of the lifeboats, mainly because of the ship's propellers revving up to pick up speed to ram the ship in high tide and afar on the beach as possible.'

Shortly, they were met by a roughly dressed man covered with grease and oil.

'Hello, how can I help you?' said the shipyard man.

'I've got you these boys for sale. Are you interested in taking them on to work for you in the shipyard or bearers in your office or home?'

'I don't think so,' he replied. 'They are too small to be of any use here in the yard. Look at that one. He can't even walk in that leg of his. That one looks like a girl. Maybe he could be sold as a dancer to dance at weddings and for men's clubs in Karachi. They are useless to me. Anyway, thank you for the offer. Now if you can excuse me, sir, I have another ship to attend to.'

He walked away, leaving the two boys and the tribal leader standing alone in a pool of old oils that covered the coastline as far as the eyes could see.

'Oh my Allah, what am I going to do with you boys now?' The old man looked upset as they made their way back to the Bedford truck.

Another year past by…

A year had passed, and everyone was talking about the invasion of Afghanistan by the Russians. Imran's imagination ran wild as he sat on a rug, listening to war stories and battle victories against the Russian infidels being told by a wild bunch of heavily armed Afghan guests to the Kuchi encampment.

He thought, *Maybe I could become a warrior if the Kochi tribe shows me how to use a gun and how to fight.* He stood up and marched across the campus, returning to sit and prune hairs around his eyebrows.

Shortly afterward, he jumped up and shouted over to Tariq, saying, 'Hey, Tariq, I want to become a soldier for jihad and Allah and fight for Islam against these infidels. I want to be like Alexander the Great or Genghis Khan and fight our Muslim enemies. How dare they, those Russians, come to our ancient homelands. These infidels must die!'

The leader looked amazed at the sudden outburst of this little young boy almost a teenager and said, 'Imran, and you too, Tariq, I'm now content in my mind that you youngsters are true believers of our Muslim faith. Yes, I also believe you are willing to die for your country and religion. Let me see where we can use your services to the best value. Tomorrow I will organize a trainer to teach you how to shoot and fight as a soldier of Allah. Let's see how it goes, and we'll wait until I hear the trainers report back to me if you are successful and learn about killing and survival skills and usage of hand grenades, rocket launchers, rocket-propelled grenades, and explosives.

'I have something to offer you that I know you will love. I am so proud of you two boys, reason being our Muslim brotherhood across the border in Afghanistan need all the help they can get to expel the Russian infidels from their homeland.'

Tariq and Imran were excited and could hardly wait to start training as a jihadist. The night seemed to take so long to finish.

At the crack of dawn, the two boys stood, washed, and got ready. Imran and Tariq learnt from his trainers that all non-Muslims were infested perverted infidels. They had no right to breathe the same air as Muslims.

Tariq reminisced, 'Oh yeah! *"Remember if they don't wish to be convert to Islam,"* they told us, *"they should be decapitated and exterminated by the sword."'*

Imran looked across at Tariq and thought, '*If that's the case, that means my mom Asahi, my sisters Neela and Sani, most of the brick-kiln workers back in Sindh should either be converted or, if they don't want to believe in the one Muslim god... Oh yes! Those Christian missionaries and those engineers and international doctors, yes, all those do-gooders... Yes! How dare they come here and try to teach us their ways! They should be killed.*

Some newspapers assumed or claimed that there was "surprisingly less" violence on the Indian side of the border during the partition, which meant that the Muslim causalities were very low. But the facts are totally different. In a letter to Gandhi (Indian independence leader), Nehru (the first prime minister of India) wrote that the Muslim casualties were twice as high in East Punjab than the Hindu and Sikh casualties collectively in West Punjab.

The British high commissioner in Karachi, estimated approximately eight hundred thousand Muslims were killed while attempting to enter into West Punjab.

According to Gyanendra Pandey (a Hindu historian), twenty thousand to twenty five thousand Muslims were massacred in Delhi. Another genocide was launched against the Muslims in Jammu and Kashmir, and countless Muslims were killed in the name of religion. It was very hard for him to comprehend. He felt sickish inside, and tears started falling from his eyes as they trickled down his cheek.

After a few hard days of training by the mujahedeen fighters, the boys were indoctrinated into the group. A small ceremony had taken place. Before long, the two boys were fully integrated without exception into the tribe of Kuchi's. They had the freedom to roam around the hilly countryside and swim whenever they wished to. They were given the role of grooming and tending to a hundred camels and additionally participated in the milking of the goats. They could take clips full of AK-47 rifle rounds and use the miniature firing range in front of a cave. They both became excellent marksmen and complimented each other for their close grouping of the rounds into the targets.

'Okay,' one would say, 'this is a Russian officer. I am going to shot him right between the eyes. Wow, great stuff,' as the bullet hit the target. Much to the excitement of the boys, they spent timeless hours practicing target shooting and bayonet drills, charging up the hills, and simulating an attack on a pretentious Russian held post.

With keen interest, the old leader watched on through his field binoculars. *It's the right decision,* he thought.

A few hours passed and before long, a heavily armed group of mujahedeen fighters and smugglers arrived from the Punjab, accompanied by a couple of well-armed white American men dressed in Khaki uniforms. They parked up a convoy of twenty civilian trucks laden with large forty-foot shipping containers on top.

Imran asked, 'Who are those white infidel men? Are they Russians?' while he squinted to block out the bright slanting sunlight from his partly open brown eyes. He pointed across at them with his right-hand index finger before dropping his arm to his side.

'They are CIA agents and American special forces. Don't worry. For the moment, they are on our side. They also want the Russians to leave Afghanistan,' said the old leader. 'They are supplying the weapons and ammunitions that are to be transferred onto the donkeys and camels backs and harnesses to trek out across the mountains by the smugglers and then across the cold, harsh threshold of the Hindi Kush terrain and beyond the border to arm the fighters of the revolution.'

The old leader said, 'To avoid Russian helicopter gunships and reconnaissance aircraft, we will travel by night and sleep in safe areas or in cleverly hidden caves during the day. Also, we will have to go down underground and travel along the subterranean water channels called Keraz. There are ventilator shafts everywhere along the route, so we can breathe easily. The Russians possibly do not know that the Kerazes exist. Therefore, we will not be noticed and we will be safe down there.

'Our sleep will regularly be disturbed whenever a group of Russian helicopter gunships fly overhead or hover. It will be nice to watch our mujahedeen fighters attack the enemy with the new Stinger missiles, especially if they are successful in shooting one or two down. It will be great to join in with mujahedeen fighters in shouts of "Allah Akbar". Our voices will echo out across the valleys. The entire trip will be dangerous, but the Kerazes are the safest and fastest way across terrain.

'We will have no reason to take unnecessary chances of being captured. These vests will ensure we don't fall into the hands of the enemy. So Tariq, step over here. We need to measure you up for you will be one of our deterrents. You will walk on the right-hand side of the caravan upfront. Therefore, if the commander instructs you to detonate the vest, this button here is all you will need to push. It is an honor to present you with this very important task. Imran, your task will be to stay with Tariq in case he is injured or, for any other reason, is unable to push the button. It will be your job to do it.'

After a restless night, Imran felt exhausted. As he rubbed his eyes and glanced out of the tent, the group of men was already out of bed, and they made haste in preparing the camel caravan and the cargo of weaponry and supplies for the dangerous journey. Morning came quickly, with the usual call to prayer recited by the head mullah.

The boys journey to Afghanistan…

Imran said, 'Come on, Tariq. It's time to get up. We are leaving soon for Afghanistan.'

Tariq shouted out, 'Oh yeah, that's right,' straightened his Salwar kameez clothing, and slipped into his sandals. 'Let's go,' he said to Imran, lifting the flap of the tent to move outside. The two boys smiled and started running over to Asif's tent.

'Are you there?' No answer.

'Oh look, there he is! Over there with the men and the camels.'

Asif seemed to sense they were looking for him. 'Hey, come on. He shouted back, waving and jumping up and down with excitement.'

Before long, the three boys were grooming the remainder of the herd of camels. 'Do you know what's in these boxes on the camel's backs?' Imran asked Asif.

'Yes, my dad showed me the new array of weapons for the mujahedeen militia.'

He went off to say as he pointed at the different casings, 'In those ones there are stinger-missile launchers. Dad said they will win the war for us and send the Russians running back to the USSR. The mujahedeen will be able to shoot down the MiG fighter jets and helicopter gunships, and only the hawks and the eagles will rule the skies over Afghanistan. In those boxes are .50 machineguns and my favorite of all. They have tracer rounds of ammunitions and range up to three kilometres. Let's go bath before breakfast for one last time.'

All three boys ran over the hilltop to the sound of the water rushing down the side of the bright green grassy slopes. 'Last in is a donkey!' shouted Asif as he approached the pool of water, already bareback with his shirt lying on the embankment. 'Come on! What's keeping you two?'

Soon all three were splashing around in the not-so-warm water, taking the time to run over the trip to Afghanistan.'

'Are you afraid what might happen to us over there?' said Asif.

'A bit, but Allah will help protect us,' said Tariq.

'Do you really believe that?' said Imran. 'My grandmother Parveen, mother, and two older sisters are Christians, and they pray to God through Jesus Christ. They say he is God's son.'

'Well then,' said Tariq, 'we will have to help if both religions are to survive.'

They laughed together as they splashed water on one another with their heads bobbing around like pieces of cork. For a moment, there was a pause, with only the hustles of feet approaching. They looked around to see who it might be, and within a few minutes, the boys were joined by the old leader and Asif's father.

'Good morning, my little warriors. Are you ready to go earn your keep and help our Afghan brothers win the war?' he said.

'Yes, please. We are as ready as can be. We didn't sleep much last night with the excitement.'

'Okay then. Let's go eat a hearty breakfast the women have cooked. They have prepared goat and roti and green tea, so eat as much as you can. Then pack the rest for the mountain pass. It's going to be cold up there,' he said as he pointed to the high peaks towering up above them.

He enquired, 'Have you two been in the mountains before?'

'No, sir, we haven't,' the boys said in harmony.

He laughed and said, 'Allah will protect you, and don't worry, it's not that scary. By the way, Tariq and Imran, my new-found sons, I have a surprise for you after breakfast.'

'Thank you, Father,' replied Imran and Tariq.

'Oh yes, for you too, Asif. I can't forget you,' he said jokingly.

The boys all wondered what the surprise might be and discussed the possibilities. But Asif stayed quiet as he had noticed his father put the presents into a box close to the entrance to the family tent that morning.

As they arrived back to the campsite, by now, all the women were gathered around the centre pivot in the campsite, a level piece of ground where most of the community used as a meeting place. The entire area was carpeted with a multitude of colored rugs.

'Today we are celebrating the arrival of the best weapons and munitions for our brothers in arms, provided by FBI, CIA, and the other USA government agencies. Most of all, we are also here to honor the thirty-five men and young boys taking the dangerous trek over one of the toughest mountain passes in the entire Hindu Kush passes.'

The boys were given the task to take water and towels around the group of men. Kicking off their sandals at the side of the rugs, they carefully stepped around the platters of food layered out across the mats. The boys had never seen such a spread or variety of delicious foods before. There were plates of chicken, goat, salads, variety of fruits and vegetables, rice, and roti bread.

'I can't wait to eat,' Imran whispered to Tariq.

They proceeded to provide the services, starting from the right. Tariq went first with the water. Followed shortly behind was Imran who carried a bundle of hand towels. After completing the job, they found a space and sat together in the large circle of people. Asif's father recited a verse from the Holy Koran and praised the courage of the mujahedeen fighters and his sons and brothers within the assemble of fine warriors. There was silence around the gathering as they each eat their fill.

As soon as the group had finished and sat around, drinking green tea, Asif's mother called out to the three boys, 'Come here, boys,' she said.

The boys asked permission form Asif's father, 'Can we please leave and go to Mom?' said Asif.

'Of course, go and give Mother a hug and take her blessing before you leave for Afghanistan.' They made their way across the uneven ground to the group of women sitting eating the remainder of the food leftovers from the men's assembly followed by the old warrior (Asif's father). Tears were falling from the compassionate old lady, and she greeted the three boys with her outstretched arms.

'Come here, my sons, and hold me one last time as maybe I will never get the chance again, at least in this world.' She looked into the three boys' eyes and said, 'Promise me you will fight the enemies of Allah with devotion and become a brave martyr and you will die and go to paradise in heaven.'

'We promise,' the boys said with a quiver in their young voices.

'Okay,' said Asif's father. 'That's enough of that. My going-away present to you boys is'—he lowered himself and opened up a wooden box, pulling out a couple of brand-new AK-47 and magazines—'here you are, Imran, Tariq, and one for you too, my son.'

The boys jumped around with joy as they grabbed and hugged. The old women called the boys back, 'I haven't given you my present,' as she picked up the parcel of US dollars belonging to Muhammad. She said, 'You will need it for your journey home after this trip as you deserve to return home to your own families. Father and I have decided it's best for you and your own parents. So as payment for helping the Afghans, get these much-needed supplies. The money, we have decided to return to you. Muhammad never owned it anyway. He got it from you two poor kids from the camel races that you risked you lives for. Now it's time to go as the journey is long, cold, and dangerous. You better keep your energy for that. Look after one another, and please, God, we will have you back soon.'

The boys thanked the old man and woman before joining up with the caravan of camels and other people and moved in a snake-like movement up the trek. Asif looked sad for the first time as he glanced back at the now-distant encampment that dotted the parched, bleached meadow, now almost bear from grazing vegetation, and said, 'The season has passed, and my community will soon depart in search of new pastures for the animals to feed on.'

Imran and Tariq felt sorry for him and said, 'We will help you find them when we get back.'

'Oh no,' Asif said. 'Don't you two understand? You will not be coming back with me. My father has made arrangements for you to be taken from Spin Boldak (Spin Boldak, Afghanistan, is less than ten kilometres from Chaman Pass), Kandahar, to Jalalabad and onto Torkham border post. Then from there, you will be able to cross the border and head down the Khyber Pass and be free to go home to your families in Pakistan.'

'Is that true?' Imran said, seeking a positive answer.

'You are good Pakistanis, but we have no room for you in our war, at least not for now. But maybe we can't beat the Russians and more countries get dragged in to a far greater war. Then you may need to fight for Pakistan.'

The terrain changed from rolling hills to short bursts of flat plains. Before long, walking became difficult as the long stretched-out caravan of camels and escorts lagged behind.

At least they had reached an asphalted roadway, but the final approach became hazardous, with the added danger of heavy traffic. Streams of refugee families nested high upon Bedford trucks and light vehicles all heading to UNHCR refugee camps being set up across Quetta, Pakistan. Other traffic heading in both directions was the Pakistani army. Surprisingly enough, no one seemed to care what they were carrying or even check their papers and cargo.

As trucks and cars sped past them, they were covered in reddish clouds of dust as they progressed along the road and the Afghan border, crossing at Chaman running through the Baluchistan Desert. The landscape gave a lunar appearance, with red rocks and high cliffs.

A vehicle slows to a stop alongside a group of our men seeking directions to Quetta and they talked to the many wounded men, their driver quietly indicated, 'Who is a mujahedeen fighter, and who is an ordinary patient?' They did it with a code if he was a patient, the driver would shake his head to indicate that "no, he is not an ordinary patient". Most of the men Imran talked to, were not real patients. (He told him later that he could pick out the fighters by their accents and demeanors. A few even confessed their allegiances, while Imran went off talking to others, before in other vehicles.

'Hey, Asif, do you know how much longer we are going to be walking before we can stop for the night?'

Asif enquired from one of the men beside him who said, 'Don't worry, we will be stopping just over there,' as he pointed out across the valley. 'The road turns over that way. Can you see the buses and trucks over there?'

'Oh yes, sir,' the boys replied.

'That's great as I don't think I can go much further today,' said Imran. Both Tariq and Asif agreed.

The road and mountains sure was colder than the boys had ever been in their lives. Tariq huddled in behind his camel in an attempt to block the wind from his face and complained to Asif and Imran. Some of the men laughed and said, 'Toughen up, you lads. This is nothing yet. Wait till we get even higher up at the Chaman Pass.'

Finally, the team leader, decided to set up camp approximately two kilometres of the road side. The fighters made great haste in erecting makeshift black traditional tents to protect everyone from the elements.

Four fighters were stationed as guards to stay awake and protect the camels and cargo from thefts or bandits. Another group of fighters, including Tariq and Imran, went off to gather up twigs and firewood. The boys were sent to shackled the front feet of their camels so that they could not run away overnight, it began to rain.

Not before long, the boys were huddled up in a blanket together in front of a blazing fire positioned just outside the front of their tent while feasting on the remainder of the food the womenfolk had prepared for their trip.

Streamlets of water gushed down the shale-like rocky slope that formed an instant river that covered the entire road. The boys didn't mind as they played with pieces of wood and watched them float away into the darkness of the night. Before long, the team leader arrived over to advise the boys to get some sleep as the border post closed at five in the afternoon and the road heading to the crossing was now jammed up with all sorts of vehicles waiting to get moving the next day into Afghanistan.

The time seemed to go so fast and it was still dark. As the boys were woken up to continue up the final kilometre to the border post. It was still raining, and everyone was saturated as they silently made their way up the winding mountain pass. They travelled in silence in order not to wake up the other people waiting to cross into Afghanistan. As arrangements were in place for them to cross under the curtain of darkness.

As they approached the post, some Pakistani border guards stood with their grey tribal shawls wrapped tightly up around their necks, the butts of their rifles protruding from under the bottom. They quietly waited under a shelter from the rain. The leader of their caravan scanned the surrounds as they approached them.

Imran went off to the side of the road and was crouched down, urinating. Tariq watched on from across the road, washed his hands in the running stream formed by the rain.

Located on a flat expanse of a roadway, Chaman border post gates built into the shape of two arches of the three-storey-high structure. A slogan 'Welcome to the frontier friendship gates, proud Pakistani'. The sign over one arch read, 'Pakistan first'.

The caravan leader said 'Okay, you must stop here and let me go talk to soldiers, to ensure we can go through.'

Some other travellers observed us and started up their vehicles, expecting the gates to open. Some of the border security shouted back at them to turn off their lights and vehicles or they would shoot them. Quickly, they followed the instruction. One driver continued to complain, 'Why are you allowed to cross through the border? Why are you so special?'

The boys were too frightened to answer. One of the guards said to him, 'Shut your mouth, or we will arrest you.'

One driver and his helper bitterly continued to complain. The leader of the caravan went over to this driver and his sidekick, saying, 'My friend,' pointing a Smith & Wesson pistol through the truck window as he stood on the sidestep. 'You, my friend,' he said as he placed the tip of the mussel of the gun onto his forehead, 'I'll kill you for money.'

He then turned the mussel of the gun at his driver, saying, 'And you, my friend, I will kill you for nothing.' The two men instantly shut up, and there was not another word from them. Both Imran and Tariq grinded and said, 'Brilliant!' and gave each other a high-five with their hands clapping in mid-air, as they danced around in a circle. Shouting "Pakistan Zinder bad.'

The driver looked frightened and quickly climbed back into his truck and closed the door.

It was not long after the leader returned smiling and said, 'We are okay to cross the border, but let's keep closer up together so they don't get tired standing in the rain and block some of us going across.'

'Also, see those ambulances coming up? They will be taking mujahedeen injured fighters across to Quetta Hospital for treatment. Some of the other injured people you see here and there with their family and friends. Most of them got blown up by landmines some others would have been from helicopter gunships.

In the meantime…

The three boys stood looking at a hill top outpost. Hay soldier can we run up there a have a look around? Asked Asif—I will ask the officer, if its ok. Replied the guard.

After a few minutes, the guard came back and said its ok but I must take you there and show you around. Promise not to steal anything or even touch anything. You are privileged to get a look around, reason been, this is a highly sensitive area. The boys were so excited.

The guard felt as if he was a tourist guide, and as they walked up the steep hillside, went on to explain to the boys. There are almost one thousand border posts placed strategically along the 1,500-mile Afghan–Pakistani border, with curfews and fences in key areas. But on the ground, one could see how easy it was for mujahedeen fighters or leaders to slip in and out.

Wow that's a lot of posts and still people can cross safely without been caught.

Yes, that's right. But others bribe the guards and they look the other way.

By now, they had reached the top. The border guards led Imran, Tariq and Arif up the dark narrow spiral staircase to the top of the observation tower where they could see Afghanistan forty or fifty feet below.

Strangely, the tower windows were all broken.

'Why was that?' asked Imran.

And the embarrassed scout from the frontier corps, with the battalion's motto 'Death Before Disgrace' clearly visible on the signboard behind his head, frowned and said, 'Sometimes the post is not manned, and the naughty Afghan goat herder boys throw stones at the windows.'

On the way, back down to the road the rain had stopped, and a brisk wind blew through the mountain.

They noticed the officer in charge come out of the office, waving his hand to the guards and pointing towards our caravan. He signalled to the guard manning the barriers to open it and let only us through.

With this, Imran ran back to help Tariq remove the shackles from the front legs of the camels and neatly place them into one of the backpacks on the saddles. Within a short period, the long line of camels, military hardware, and equipment cargo were walked across the barrier by the rest of the men who had entered 'no man's land'.

The plan to stay in between had been changed as the Pakistani officers demanded we go straight through without stopping, not even to stop for toilet purposes. Their guards were under strict orders to open fire on anyone who breaks the rule or anything that moves.'

As they passed under the barrier Imran and Tariq started smiling and said to each other, 'Great, we are in Afghanistan.'

Asif said, 'Oh no, we still have about one or two hundred metres more to go, before we enter Afghanistan.

This is called "no man's land". It stretches out in both directions along the entire Pakistan and Afghan border. It then joins up to continue along the borderline of Iran to the left and India to the right-hand side'

Up ahead they could see another barrier, what is that for? Asked Imran.

Before anyone could answer and as they came closer to a barrier, a shout came from behind it, and a number of torches pointed at the boys and other men. 'Afghani militiamen—they were manning a border post. Nobody had informed them that we were coming,' said the leader, 'so don't move until I get clearance.'

The militiamen were heavily armed with rocket-propelled grenades and AK-47s at the ready, and more soldiers were seated high up on their armored military vehicles. The scene was tense. Over the noise, one could hear the occasional clatter of automatic gunfire or the thud of a mortar-shell explosion, a way off in the distance.

Tariq said, 'Hey, Imran, are you afraid yet?'

'Hmmm, I think so. But not sure. But there is no turning back. I think the mujahedeen would shoot us if we tried to run away now. Just pray to Allah for us to gain some extra bravery and suspend the pain of war.'

As soon as they noticed we were carrying weapons and supplies for the mujahedeen, shouts of delight were accompanied with warm hugs from the guards manning the post.

Before long, they were all across and told that they had to move to the other side of the road as in Afghanistan, they drove on the right-hand side of the road. There too, traffic was back up and appeared to be much heavier than on the Pakistani side, everyone was sleeping and as they slowly passed, some babies could be heard crying for a feed, from their sleeping mothers.

The leader explained to the boys, that most of these people were refugees waiting to escape from the fighting in the towns and villages.

'Okay, stop and wait here,' said the leader as he walked backwards to the rest of the men and informed them to join him at the front of the long caravan of camels for instructions. As they all gathered around, he explained, 'From here onwards, we are leaving the roadway and will camp up for the day. But before we go to sleep, we must pray, tend to the animals, have food, prepare tents.'

Imran said to Tariq and Asif, 'My feet are very sore. I am very cold, and still we have some distance to travel before we rest.'

'Stop complaining, said a big mujahedeen fighter.' They laughed out loud before being told to shut up.

Morning brought with it a bright sunny day, much to the delight of everyone, especially on the boys' faces. Smiles and good spirit brought back their enthusiasm.

Before long, they reached the first wayward point and the first of many on the way to Spin Boldak Town.

'Do you know how many days it's going to take to get to Spin Boldak?' asked Tariq.

'I think if things go well, approximately another day or so, that is, weather permitting and, of course, Russian activities along our route. But we are not too worried about the ground forces as they are not down this far as yet. Okay, groups of special forces can arrive in the helicopters and MiG jets—that's the main problem. They can appear at a moment's notice and won't care whom they kill.'

'Stop that kind of talk. We are going to be okay,' said Tariq with a look of concern on his face.

On arrival at the resting post, they noticed there was a small tea shop serving hot green tea.

'Hey, Imran, can we spend some of those dollars and get everyone green tea and kebabs?'

'Please shut up, Tariq. Don't broadcast we have a huge some of the money as these people would kill their own mother for it.' Best if we just go without.

'Sorry, Imran,' said Tariq. 'You are right.'

Hay boy's tomorrow morning, said the leader. 'we have a class in explosives ordinance reconnaissance. This will teach you as what is safe to do and what not to touch for your own safety and that of your brothers. Most of the region stretching from Kandahar Province up to Herat Province is covered by minefields. For this very reason, a lot of our intended journey will be traversed through the network of mountain caves and underground passageways water courses called Karezes. The Russian military engineers have peppered the terrain with anti-personnel mines (cluster bombs) and anti-tank mines. Moreover, plenty more mines have been dropped by the Russian infidel flying war machines from the skies'.

Sir, Tariq and I have decided to stay with you and the other men. We can always go to Pakistan later. Oh, great said the leader and a friendly cheer from the group endorsed his decision to let they stay.

He then said to the boys. Ok then, back to study as this stuff will save your lives in this neck of the woods.

'These cluster bombs are designed to attract the interest of the unassuming people and mujahedeen fighters. Some explode it lifted-up off the ground, some explode when walked upon, others can explode for no reason at all. They are filled with fine particles of fibreglass, when they enter the body they travel through the veins to finally reach the heart and kill the victim. The international community have asked for them to be totally band from usage in areas especially where civilians are living'.

'So to get our shipment safely to its destination, we have a duty to perform, and time is not an issue. the closest point or roadway is not always the one that we take as we will be guided and recommended by our CIA international intelligence sources with reliable information they get via US military satellites. This means we will have to take the longer routes to our destination if we are to supply the front lines with the powerful new weapons.'

The course was held in a tent facilitated by a US soldier dressed in local costume and translator from the mujahedeen ex-Afghan army ordinance officer.

Few nights later…

Travelling by night and sleeping by day. 'Hey, Asif, do you know how much longer are we going to be walking before we can stop for a sleep?'

Asif didn't know the answer, so he enquired from one of the mujahedeen fighters walking along beside him who replied, 'Don't you boys be worried. We will be stopping just over there. It should take us another hour to reach that,' as he pointed out across the valley. 'Do you see the signage for the turn off straight over there?'

'Oh yes, sir. I can see that distant road where the buses and trucks are turning off over there,' replied Tariq.

'Oh yes, sir,' the boys replied. 'That's great as I don't think I can go much further today,' said Imran. Both Tariq and Asif agreed.

Before long, they reached the first wayward point and the first of many on the way to Spin Boldak Town.

'Do you know how many days it's going to take to get to Spin Boldak?' asked Tariq.

Hay Tariq 'Stop complaining, or I will hand you over to the Russian infidels. They will feed you to their wives and children for dinner,' a large bearded mujahedeen fighter said jokingly. The majority of the fighters laughed out loud before being told to shut up by the same bearded person.

A short distance had passed by, and before long, the animals and every one of the team had settled down for the day. It was hard at first to sleep, listening to the warlike sounds echoing from afar and the rumbling of the passing vehicles along the highway from Chaman to Spin Boldak. Whatever happened next, the entire caravan passed in slumber land and were fast asleep.

The early evening Tuesday brought with it a beautiful, full-moonlit night. Funnily enough, it was strange waking to darkness, and travel from here on would be in darkness.

Tariq said to Imran, 'How are you feeling tonight?'

'I dreamt of my father and mother. I hope that they are not missing me too much. As my father used to say, if you dream about someone, they are thinking of you too. But I will forget about that dream now as after surviving my first few days inside Afghanistan territory and am still alive, they have nothing to worry about.'

Much to the delight of everyone, especially on the boys' faces, smiles, a good feed of meat, hot tea, and good spirits brought back their enthusiasm.

Shortly along the road, they were guided by radio again to take the steep hill track which was located at the right-hand side of the road. From there, it was easy to hide the consignment of weapons from any Russian helicopter gunships that might happen to be patrolling the skies.

They pushed ahead. After two days, they could reach the township of Spin Boldak. The town was crowded with hundreds—maybe thousands—of refugee families and people bedding down for the night. They steadily passed along through the side roads under the guidance of many different mujahedeen fighters.

For this part of the journey, they were advised to break up into small groups of two or three camels, just in case of informers passing on information to the enemy Russian soldiers. They regrouped on the other side of the town. We were guided to a countryside Keraz (underground water way), the first underground canal system. Hoists were used to lower the camels and equipment down the short distance to the bottom of the shaft-like entrance.

Next, it was their turns to sit on the hoist rope, and gently, they were lowered into the rush of the cold passing canal water. At this point it covered both Imran and Tariq up to the waist. The entrance was well lighted, with Tilley lamps and other torches and candles. They had been given head torches with straps to hold them on their heads.

As they walked along through the tunnels, they were instructed to turn off the torches as they approached the openings leading to the top. The shafts were positioned approximately fifty to one hundred metres apart. They travelled underground in the water for three to four hours. The cave-like tunnels were high enough for the camels and equipment to pass without hinder from the rocky canopy above. The leader asked Tariq and Imran if they were tired and wanted to sit up on the camels. Both agreed it would be nice. The leader of the group told one of the mujahedeen fighters to help the boys get settled.

The leader stated, 'God willing, if we are lucky, it will only take one or two days onwards to Kandahar City.

The guide stopped the caravan near to a shaft. He used a rope to climb up the sidewall to the opening at the top. He did this in total darkness. He checked to see if there were any signs of the enemy. The coast was clear, and he beckoned the others to start climbing up to the surface.

Next night, they had dinner with a local group of Afghan nomads and their families. They prayed for their safe passage to Herat City and successful fight to free Afghanistan from the Russian infidels.

They were introduced to a local mujahedeen fighter who was to be our guide as we crossed over the vast expanses of the dusty desert of Farah Province. He said it was expected to take about three to four days, depending on the health of our camels and fighters. There were hardly any obstacles such as Russian forces in great numbers or garrisons. All their outposts were identified and highly likely to be under attack by the regional mujahedeen fighters. This was cleverly organized as decoy to get the shipment through to the destination without being detected. For the most part, the Russians mainly travelled by helicopters and recon aircraft.

Night five of the journey…

But they achieved it in just two days. They made a detour around the west of Shindand. The Russians would be out in force there because of a reasoned attack on the Herat Airport as they had a very large air-force base there.

Bypassing the Herat Airport, we crossed over the Hari Rudd River bridge Pul-e Malan on the right, and with the aid of the local mujahedeen, we cascaded through the narrow laneways all the way into the city of Herat.

Back in the Thar Desert…

Parveen was still asleep, or was she?

'Come on. Get up. It's late, Mother, and we have slept in this morning.' Mushtaq headed out the front door of the tiny house to prepare for ablution. 'Come on, Caleb. Let's get ready for morning prayers.'

'Okay, Father. I am coming.'

Mushtaq stopped in his tracks and said to himself, 'That's strange. Mother (Parveen) didn't answer me.' So he shouted out again to her to get up. By this time, his wife Asahi had finished preparing breakfast.

'Can you please go wake Parveen?' he requested.

'Come on, Grandma,' said Asahi. 'It's time to get out of bed as breakfast is ready.'

But no reply came from Grandma's bedroom. As Caleb and his mother approached her bed, they noticed Grandma was sitting, holding on to her chest. She struggled to get her breath.

'What's wrong, Parveen?'

Mushtaq had just entered the room and ran over to help his mother. 'Oh, Mommy, what's wrong with you? Do you have a pain in your chest?'

'Oh no, Son. It's… Imran,' she said. 'Imran… I think he's alive, and I had a very pleasant surprise he came home to us.'

'Stop it. You just had a dream. Now pull yourself together,' said Mushtaq.

'Mushtaq, please forgive me as I gave Imran away to two men.'

'What are you saying, Mother (Parveen)?'

'Yes, it's true, and I am ashamed of myself.'

'I can't imagine that you've done this terrible deed to my son,' said Mushtaq.

She replied, 'Really, I have been sick to death, carrying the burden around.'

'Why, Mother? Why? For what purpose?' said Mushtaq.

'They told me they would give me twenty-five thousand rupees. The men told me to trust them as they would bring back the money to me at the chapel. But when they never returned, I had to made up a story. My seizure was genuine. I think it cured because of the shock of losing both as I was afraid to face you and the family as I had lost both Imran and the money,' said Parveen.

'Where did they take him?' said Mushtaq.

'I don't know, but they were educated people. I believe they would teach him a trade or give him employment,' said Parveen.

'How did they get him to go with them as I always warned him about strangers?' said Mushtaq.

'The men gave me some medicine to give Imran. I walked him around until he fell asleep. We put Imran into a car. They promised to come back, and they also said Imran will have a better life where he was going. I did ask them where they were taking Imran. They just pointed down the road, but there was another little boy sleeping in the back seat, and they put Imran in the car beside him,' said Parveen.

'Why did you do this?'

'We needed the money, and I wanted to pay off the Malik and take us all back to Kamoke Town or somewhere in the Punjab. I planned to buy a small plot of land to build a little house with your help, and we as a family could live happy up there. I was going to sell the camel back then too. The money for her, we could have travelled by train as that was always a dream of mine—to take you all on a trip by train. Trains are in our blood,' she said.

'I can't believe you did this to my precious son Imran,' said Mushtaq.

His wife Asahi stood motionless on the floor in a state of shock, listening to the bad news unfold. She too, grieving, carried the burden of the disappearance of her little eight-year-old son so many years before.

'Oh my god,' said Parveen.

Asahi stood, looking puzzled. 'How could you do this to me?' Asahi said as she finally cried out.

'I am very sorry, Asahi, but I felt back then that maybe it would be good for us and Imran too.'

'Okay then. Now that we are starting to get the facts out in the open,' said Mushtaq, 'is the Malik truly my father?' asked Mushtaq.

'Yes, but we didn't have a real relationship back then. He raped me and my sister Bulbul,' said Parveen.

'How do you expect to believe you did not want to have sex with him after the story you held back about Imran for all these years, living as if he were dead?' asked Mushtaq.

'You must believe me, my son,' said Parveen.

'He and his friends forced us to do it with them. Why don't you go ask him if he is your father or not?' said Parveen.

'Okay, I will,' Mushtaq said as he bust open the door and went straight over to the Malik's house, shouting, 'Malik! Where are you? Get out here now! I want to talk to you.'

The Malik's gardener was busy putting away the gardening tools in the garden shed. He looked surprised as he stumbled over to the door and replied, 'What is the problem? What do you want? Did you not see the family go in the car on Thursday? You were standing just over there. Anyway, the Malik Saab is not here. He had gone to Karachi for the weekend with his wife and family. He will not be back until tomorrow afternoon,' said the gardener.

'Where in Karachi?' asked Mushtaq.

'His house is in the Clifton District, facing out towards the Arabian Sea. I can give you the address but only if it's very important. But first, I must call him and make sure he doesn't mind me giving it to you,' said the gardener.

'Oh yes, it's very important. Okay,' said Mushtaq. 'Thanks.'

Parveen stood at the door of her tiny house, with the girls Sani and Neela, and they watched as Mushtaq and the gardener chatted. She had a look of total despair on her face while Imran's mother Asahi cried, clutching on to Caleb for comfort.

'He is too young to understand the situation,' said Asahi to herself.

Parveen said to herself, 'What have I done to my family?'

She stood motionless and trembling in her shoes while clutching on to her holy rosary beads, flickering a bead at a time through her fingers and muttering a prayer under her breath.

Shortly afterwards, Mushtaq returned and told his wife he was going to Karachi in the morning.

'Please don't,' she cried. 'Forget about it.'

'Okay, then how do you think I feel? That bastard, treating me and our family as slaves while, all the time, we are family! He is going to pay us for the hardship caused to my mother and our kids.'

Mushtaq stayed there briefly before returning to the Malik's house to meet up with the gardener again.

'We will get him. You give us enough money to get out of this misery. Yes, we will go to Kamoke and have a decent-like style. At least we can have our girls home on long weekends and school holidays, and Caleb can go to a fine school,' said Parveen to Asahi.

'Hello, is that you, Malik?' said the Malik's gardener as he stood inside the parlor, holding the phone to his right ear.

'Yes, it is,' said the deep voice on the other end of the telephone line. Why did you call me?'

'I just wanted to warn you that Mushtaq came to the house and was mad with rage over something,' said the gardener.

'What did he say or wanted?' asked the Malik.

'He did not say, but I gave him your address as it seemed to be important, and I just wanted to let you know he intends to come see you at your Karachi residence tomorrow morning.'

'Oh no, why did you give it to him? Okay then, the damage is done. Go get him over to talk to me on the phone,' said the Malik.

'Okay, Saab. I will go get him from his house.'

A few minutes passed by, Mushtaq sat on a chair, smoking a cigarette on the front veranda as he noticed the gardener approach.

'Excuse me, Mushtaq. I have just spoken to the Malik in Karachi. He wants to talk to you on his house phone. Can you please come with me?'

Mushtaq stood up and followed the gardener down the road and into the Malik's house. Both men were standing, looking at the phone as it rang out.

Mushtaq lifted the phone, and he said in a sarcastic loud tone of voice, 'Hello, Dad, and how are you, you bastard? Oh yes, I know the truth, and it's going to be broadcast to the neighbors. Mom, yes, Parveen told me everything. Oh yes, everyone is going to know very shortly.'

To Mushtaq, there was a scary silence on the other end of the phone as the Malik held on tightly to the phone receiver before holding his breath and stared up at the ceiling.

'Well then, Son, where do we go from here?' said the Malik.

Mushtaq replied, 'Now the only people who know the full story are your loyal gardener servant, my mother Parveen, my wife, and your little grandson Caleb.'

'Well, that's good,' said the Malik. 'Let's keep it that way. I am coming back to my house tomorrow. So you do not need to travel to Karachi. My wife and sons are here and will be staying another week. Let's come to some settlement, and I intend to pay you a healthy sum of money, but only if my wife and family do not find out the truth.'

'Okay,' said Mushtaq, 'sounds like a very good plan. Oh yes, there is another thing. My mother will be wanting to hear from you what happened to her sister Bulbul that night you and your friend raped them both,' said Mushtaq.

'How did you know about that?' said the Malik.

'It's the rumors circulating through the brick-kiln workers. I happened to overhear that you murdered Bulbul,' said Mushtaq.

'My dear son, that's only a rumor. Bulbul, yes, was in my father's house that night, but no, we did not kill her or burn her body on the brick-kiln,' the Malik went on to say. 'Your auntie Bulbul escaped from our family house, and from what I understand, she is safe, living in the Punjab with another family friend of my father. She, like Parveen, is also a grandmother too.'

Mushtaq shouted, 'So you want me to believe that too? Oh, so from you and your mate's drunken night at your father's house, she managed to escape. How would she find a way in the dark and alone as a woman?'

'That night, my father returned from Karachi. He brought his friend who was a single man who was looking for a wife. They went searching for Bulbul and found her wandering down the desert track. My father drove through the night with his friend and Bulbul. A few days later, they were married, and the rest is history.'

'I don't believe you, Malik,' said Mushtaq.

'Oh yes, Mushtaq,' said the Malik. 'She really is married. My dad's friend and she had two children of their own. Tomorrow, when I return home, I will give your mother the address in the morning. Let's all meet in my house to settle this once and for all.'

'Okay,' said Mushtaq. 'I hope that you are not playing games with my head. I will go back and tell Parveen about our conversation.

Mushtaq then thanked the old gardener and said it's in his best interest not to go around talking about what he heard just now on the phone.

The old gardener outreached his trembling hand and humbly shook Mushtaq's and, in a low voice, said, 'My dear fellow, I am delighted you found out that the Malik is your father. I have known the true story since you were born. The old Malik—peace be upon him and his soul—he also knew.'

The old gardener tried to ease the pain he could see in Mushtaq's face and invited him to drink tea with him and talk about the reasons the Malik never had shown his love towards Parveen or even towards him growing up.

The gardener passed a cup of tea over the kitchen table and went on to say, 'Mushtaq, you know, back then, when your mother Parveen and the Malik had an affair—'

'It was not an affair,' said Mushtaq. 'It was forced sex. It was rape.'

'That's not right. They had a secret love affair together. That night, your auntie Bulbul arrived over to the Malik's house. I was working on the tube well, waiting on the quota of water to finalize. When I looked over towards the brick kiln, your auntie and Parveen were shouting and arguing about something. I could not hear, but clearly, they were upset.

'Parveen, your mother, then came here to this very kitchen. The Malik was here, drinking alcohol with his friends. The Malik brought her upstairs to his room. Shortly afterwards, Bulbul came rushing past, shouting vulgar words at the top of her voice. She ran upstairs and seemly caught your mother and the Malik in bed. Before long, she was screaming and running out of the house and down the dusty track towards town. After a short while, the Malik's father—'peace be upon him'—came home with his friend in the family car. The rest of the story is what I explained to you earlier.'

Mushtaq listened in silence.

'Please don't be sad, Mushtaq,' said the old gardener. 'I know it was a hard life, but the Malik really does love your mother. But unfortunately, within our society, if the community discovered they had an affair out of holy wedlock, every one of us would suffer. You, your mother, and even the children might even be killed. I am sure you understand that as a fact of life here in Pakistan. It would be different across the border in India.'

Mushtaq murmured and twisted on the chair. 'I am so confused and feel like everyone around here knew about it.'

'No,' said the old gardener. 'Can you imagine the struggle they both endured, meeting in secret places to share their love for each other and private moments together? But it all ended when your mother gave birth to you. Both of their lives became almost unbearable, especially when the Malik's father discovered the baby was his son's. He tried to get your mother to leave to one of the Christian convents until she had you. But your mother would not go. She created an imaginary father in her head. She was so convincing that the illiterate community of brick workers believed her or maybe just didn't want to get involved. Therefore, she told everyone your father had died in the Punjab just before she arrived here with your auntie Bulbul.

'The Malik told his father about it, and he forbade his son to see your mother. He sent him off to live in Karachi, and the family quickly arranged a marriage with his current wife. I too suffered to see him pretend to like or love his new wife. The flame still burns in his heart for your mother, even after all these years.

'I still remember your real father, the Malik, standing here at this very window, looking out across at the brick pits. Clearly, he was deeply in love with your mother back then. She was a beautiful young lady too, full of life and charm,' said the old gardener. 'Before he departed, I noticed a tear in his eye. But truly, I believe he still loves your mother and longed for the day he could—I think, this day—talk to you about it.

He always discussed with me about how messed up his life had become since his teenage days when he was having an affair and fell in love with your mother.

'She always had long conversations with him as to how she loved Kamoke Village and the railway people living there. Yes, she longed to be able to return there with you, Mushtaq, your wife Asahi, and the four children. So please, I would ask you to consider this when you meet tomorrow, no matter what you think or believe. He is a broken man,' said the old gardener.

Mushtaq again shook the gardener's hand then quietly went out of the Malik's house and stood on the veranda, facing the well-manicured gardens. As he stood there, he admired the roses and the fragrance of a jacaranda tree. He lit up a cigarette while taking a drag and walked over towards the running tube well; water was in full flow. He thought, *Gee, how hard a struggle we have had here. How selfish a man this person is, whom they are telling me is my father.*

He peered across at the dimly light shambles of a house his mother and her sister Bulbul had built with their bare hands. He thought, *Just imagine, they were children about the same age as Sani and Neela are now.*

He studied how steadily the workers were walking on top of the hot brick stacks. His imagination started to be bounced around with ideas as to how he could profit from the outcome of tomorrow's meeting with the Malik.

'Can't believe it,' he said to himself. 'This man is my father.'

He takes his last look back at the wealthy crops standing high and out across the distant fields, the lights shining so brightly from the house and gardens.

Mushtaq quietly and slowly moved back home before he paused to douse out his cigarette under his foot. He knocked on the front door, and before anyone inside could call out 'Who's there?' he entered the room. He compared the two houses—the Malik's with tube lights and their house dimly lit up from small Tilley lamps hanging from the ceiling.

'Hey, Mother and Asahi,' said Mushtaq as he stepped over the children sitting on the mat on the floor. 'Come here quickly as I have fantastic news for you both, in fact, for the whole family.' He stopped to catch his breath.

'Yes,' said Mushtaq. 'I have just had a conversation with the Malik Saab by phone to Karachi. Bulbul is alive and well. She is married and has two children with two grandkids of her own and lives in her own house.

'Where is she living? Is she living close by? Is she coming here? I want to go see her now. Why did she not come back to help us escape from here?' said an excited Parveen.

'She lives in the Punjab with her extended family. It's too far away to go. Let's wait and see. I am meeting with the Malik tomorrow to talk about our future. Just wait and see. Also, I am going to demand he send some people to find our son Imran,' replied Mushtaq.

Parveen cried out loud and fell on her knees, clapped her two hands together before she jumped up again with excitement, and hugged and jumped around with delight. Mushtaq, Asahi, and their children never saw Grandma so happy like this in their lives before.

'Oh, what a night,' said Mushtaq.

'All we need now is our Imran back, and we can all move to the Punjab. At least there was some hope that Imran may return home someday. as this is 1991' he will be eleven years old now, Parveen had the nerve to say. She sighed and said, 'Everything is going to be all right tomorrow,' as Imran's mother and father agreed with her.

The kids Caleb, Sani, and Neela were still puzzled as to what all the crying and fuss was about. Asahi, Parveen, and the three children huddled up tightly together and knelt on the floor in front of the picture of Jesus. Mushtaq recited a verse of the Koran. He said, out loud its 'almost tomorrow'. The family sat around and prayed in unity together.

Glossary

Anarkali Bazaar

The Anarkali Bazaar (stated to be more than 250 years) is the oldest bazaar of Lahore, Pakistan. It sells textiles, garments, jewellery, and many other items. Anarkali Bazaar is divided into two portions—the old Anarkali Bazaar and the new Anarkali Bazaar. The old Anarkali Bazaar is noted for traditional food items, while the new Anarkali Bazaar is noted for its traditional handicraft and embroidery cloths.

Anglo-Indian

The Anglo-Indian community in India is mostly urban and Christian and traces its origin to the earliest contact between Europe and India, ultimately to 1498, when Portuguese navigator

Bangalore

Bangalore is the capital of the southern state of Karnataka, India, and is Asia's fastest growing cosmopolitan city. The city is blessed with great climate, gardens, parks, natural lakes, architectural landmarks, shopping malls and is home to the best restaurants.

The British army designed (Bangalore Torpedo) an explosive pipe for clearance of barbed wire or low wire-entanglement fences in World War I.

Bull-Pit Brick Kiln

It is designed by Captain
Bull in 1887 and is still
widely used in the brick-
manufacturing industry
to this very day.

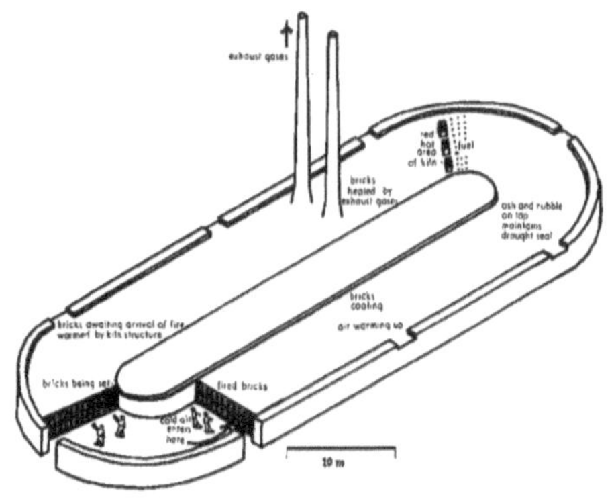

Charpoy (Charpoy or Charpie)

It is a wooden village-style bed. *Char* means 'four', *pai* means 'bed'—in
other words, 'four-legged bed'. The upper portion is a matted rope
intertwined to form the seat or laying part. There are special ends for
the feet and head. Traditionally, the bed is never left standing on the
end meant for one's head. Muslims face the head portions of the bed
in the direction towards Mecca while sleeping as a symbol of respect
for Allah.

It is designed by Captain Bull in 1887 and is still widely used in the
brick-manufacturing industry to this very day.

Daal

Dal (also spelled *daal*) is an Indian and Pakistani dish. It is essentially
a part of the family daily consumption, lentils, peas, and beans; also
used for various soups prepared from these pulses; are amongst the
most important staple foods in South Asia; and form an important
part of Indian, Nepali, Pakistani, Sri Lankan, and Bangladeshi cuisine.
Dal are frequently eaten with flatbreads, such as roti's or chapattis, or
with rice. Dals is high in protein.

Environmental Protection Authorities (EPA)

It is a practice of protecting the natural environment on individual, organisation-controlled, or governmental levels for the benefit of both environment and humans. Because of the pressures of overconsumption, population, and technology, the biophysical environment is being degraded, sometimes permanently. This has been recognized, and governments have begun placing restraints on activities that cause environmental degradation. Since the 1960s, activity of environmental movements has created awareness of the various environmental issues. There is no agreement on the extent of the environmental impact of human activity and even scientific dishonesty occurs, so protection measures are occasionally debated.

Ferozsons Bookstore

Located in Mall Road, Lahore, Pakistan, Ferozsons Bookstore was established in 1894 by Maulvi Faros-ul-Din, first owner and founder of Ferozsons. He started his work by publishing and printing the books in Lahore.

Frankincense

It is a substance that is burned for its sweet smell that was used in religious ceremonies in ancient times.

Kamoke

Kamoke is a town of Gujranwala District located in Punjab, Pakistan. It has a population of 167,300. The city is the capital of Kamoke Tehsil which is an administrative subdivision of the district. The city is itself is subdivided into eight union councils. The city is located on the Grand Trunk Road, twenty-one kilometres from Gujranwala and forty-four kilometres from Lahore.

Kuchi people

The nomads and semi-nomads, generally called Kuchi in Afghanistan, mostly keep camel, sheep, goats and Kuchi dogs. They live on animal meat, dairy products, hair and wool is used to barter or sold in order to get grain, vegetables, fruit and other products from settled people in villages and towns.

In this way, an extensive network of exchange has developed along the main routes annually followed by the nomads. The Pashtuns used to move annually from the Afghanistan mountains to the valley of the Indus. These long-distance migrations were stopped during the early 60s when the border with Afghanistan and Pakistan were closed. Again, with the war in Afghanistan a number of the nomads settled in Pakistan as the Russians killed many, as they believed they were smuggling weapons to the mujahedeen. Both governments agreed nomadic people are exempt and allowed to cross as border. Most border officials recognize the Kuchi migrations which occur seasonally and allow them to pass even in times of political turmoil. In recent decades, migrations inside Afghanistan continues, although trucks are now often being used to take livestock and extended-families from one grazing area to another."

Laddu (Traditional Sweet)

Laddu or *laddoo* are ball-shaped sweets. Laddus are made of flour, minced dough, and sugar, with various other ingredients that vary by recipe and taste. They are often served at festive or religious ceremonies, in India, Pakistan and Bangladesh.

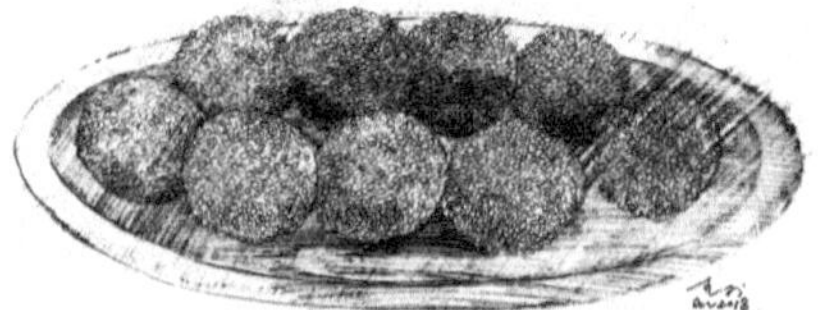

Lahore Junction or Central Railway Station

Lahore Junction Station was constructed by Mian Mohammad Sultan Chagatai, a former official of the Mughal Empire, between 1859 and 1860. The station served as the headquarters for the Punjab Railway and later would serve as the northern terminus of the Sindhi, Punjab, and Delhi Railway, which connected the port city of Karachi to Lahore. It was built in the style of a medieval castle to ward off any potential future uprisings as seen in the 1857 War of Independence, with thick walls, turrets, and holes to direct gun and cannon fire for defense of the structure. It remains a legacy of the extensive railway network established during the British Raj and reflects the British contribution to the region's infrastructure. The station was severely affected during the riots which followed the partition of the British Indian Empire and the independence of Pakistan in 1947. Similar to the contemporaneous situation with migrating Muslims from Delhi, Lahore's Hindus and Sikhs migrating to India were frequently attacked and killed in large numbers.

Line of Control

The term *line of control (LoC)* refers to the military control line between the Indian and Pakistani controlled parts of the former princely state of Jammu line which, to this day, does not constitute a legally recognized international boundary but is the de facto border. Originally known as the Cease-fire Line, it was re-designated as the 'line of control', following the Shimla Agreement which was signed on 3 July 1972. The part of the former princely state that is under Indian control is known as the state of Jammu and Kashmir. The two parts of the former princely state that are under Pakistani control are known as Gilgit–Baltistan and Azad Kashmir (AJK). Its northernmost point is known as the NJ9842.

Malik

In local communities in Pakistan and India, they are held high in society and are normally large property owners or businessmen in local communities in Pakistan and India. It is normally used as *Malik Saab*.

Mataucha Reyna

An army general in Northeast India from 1942 to 1944, Mataucha Reyna was born in Saga prefecture and adopted by the Mataucha family. He graduated from the military academy in 1910 as an infantry officer. He graduated from the army staff college in 1917 and served with the Siberian expedition.

A member of the 'Imperial Way' faction, Mataucha was the regiment commander over the units involved in the Marco Polo incident of 7 July 1937, and his arrogance helped launched the second Sino-Japanese War. He believed that weakness was provocative and rapidly escalated what was originally a minor local skirmish. Well-connected politically, he was subsequently promoted to major general and held numerous responsible staff assignments in China and Manchuria.

Mataucha was given command of *18 Division* in April 1942. His division participated in the Malaya offensive during the early months of the war, and he was wounded in the shoulder during the final assault on Singapore in February 1942. The division was then transferred to the Philippines to assist in the reduction of Bataan. By April 1942, it was on the move again, this time, to Rangoon.

Mataucha was given command of *15 Army* in March 1943. Impressed with the accomplishments of army, he strongly pushed his own plan to attack Imphal forwards.

Mountbatten

Francis Albert Victor Nicholas Mountbatten, first Earl Mountbatten of Burma, was born as Prince Louis of Battenberg on 25 June 1900. On 27 August 1979, he was known informally as Lord Mountbatten.

He was the last viceroy of India in 1947 and the first governor general of the independent Dominion of India from 1947 to 1948.

In 1979, Mountbatten, his grandson Nicholas, and two others were killed by the Provisional Irish Republican Army (IRA) which had placed a bomb in his fishing boat '*Shadow V*' in Ireland.

Muhammad Ali Jinnah (Quaid-E-Azam)

Born in Karachi, British India, and died on 11 September 1948 in Karachi, Pakistan, he was the first governor general of Pakistan from 14 August 1947 to 11 September 1948.

Murree Brewery Pakistan

The Murree Brewery Company Ltd. was established in 1860 to meet the beer demand of British personnel at Ghora Gali District, near the resort place of Murree.

Types; Murree beers, vodka, whiskey etc.

The Brewery was managed by the family of Edward Dyer. In the 1880s, the company established a further brewery in Rawalpindi and a distillery in Quetta.

Because of scarcity of water in Murree in the 1920s, brewing was mostly transferred to Rawalpindi, but malting continued at Ghora Gali until the 1940s when this property was sold. This brewery built in the Gothic style of architecture was burnt during the independence of Pakistan in 1947.

Ravi River

The Ravi waters rise in the majestic Himalayas in the Indian State of Himachal Pradesh and continue by turning southwest at the Jammu and Kashmir border. The river then flows into Pakistan and, after running a course of 50 miles (approximately 80 kilometres), enters the Punjab Province past Lahore, navigating west where it joins up with the Chenab River, with a total course of 450 miles (725 kilometres).

After the partition of India in 1947, the rivers of Ravi, along with others in the Indus system, were divided amongst the countries as per the Indus Water Treaty. The Indus Basin Project was subsequently taken up by Pakistan, while many inter basis transfers like irrigation, hydropower, and several multipurpose projects were built in the Indian territory.

Russian Invasion of Afghanistan (December 1979 February 1989)

In 1979 as Russian forces rushed into Afghanistan with their super-power military might. The Soviet Union's invasion into Afghanistan was on the pretence that Mr. Amin's government had asked them for help. Thousands of Afghans joined the mujahedeen, a guerrilla force who declared a jihad—a holy war or a mission for Allah. Their aim was to overthrow the Amin government. To counteract this action, the Soviets tried to use their overwhelming power to support the Amin government.

As same month Amin was shot by the Soviets and he was replaced by Kamal a puppet for the invaders. During the time, a variety of skilled Afghan soldiers deserted from the army and joined the mujahedeen and the Kamal government needed an estimated ninety thousand heavily armed troops to assist him to stay in power. It was stated at the time that the army's objective was to support a legitimate government and that the mujahedeen were terrorists and Russian soldiers would exterminate them. But much to the surprise many a Russian soldier also joined the mujahedeen fighters and fought alongside them against their own brothers.

As winter approached in 1982 most of the country was under the control of the mujahedeen. Young Russian conscript soldiers, were no match against men fuelled by their religious belief from despite fighting the might of the world's second most powerful military power. Soviet military hardware such as tanks were of little use in the mountain passes. Same goes for their helicopters and fighter jets in the skies, as with the introduction of the Stinker Missile Rocket Launcher supplied by the US of A they too became easy targets. Before long, the biggest export from Afghanistan, was body bags with the cream of Russians youth shipped back home. In February1989 with the Soviets economy in tatters and a military force on its knees the leaders of the USSR made a hasty withdrawal after deciding to call it a day. Moreover, with the convoy of 'vehicles of shame' thundering out across the Amu River Bridge. To the echoes of the Afghans people shouting victory and singing songs of praises to Allah, the bear with its tale between its legs exited Afghanistan, never to return.

Saab

In Urdu, Punjabi, and Hindi languages, this means 'gentlemen'. It is commonly used with a 'G' in front of it, which means 'good gentlemen'. The feminine version of *Saab* means 'madam gentle-woman'.

Sindh

Also spelled *Sind* or *Shind*, it is a province of Southeast Pakistan. It is bordered by the provinces of Baluchistan and Punjab.

Sitar Instrument

It is a traditional string instrument typically used for weddings and other ceremonies throughout Sindh, of Indian origins.

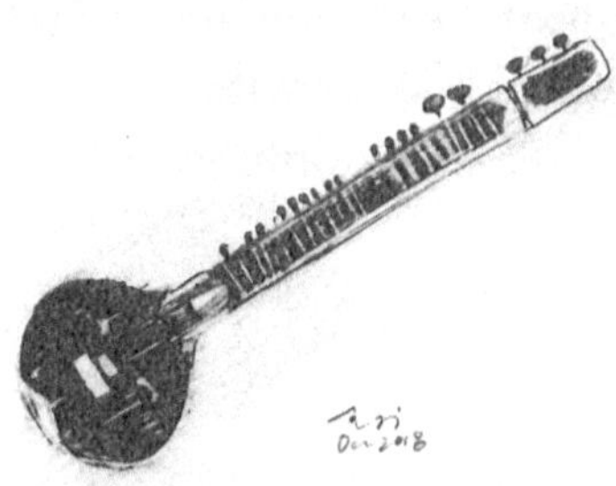

Tabla Drum Set

The Tabla Drums are the most popular of all the traditional drums, typically used for weddings and other ceremonies throughout Sindh Province, Pakistan, India and Bangladesh.

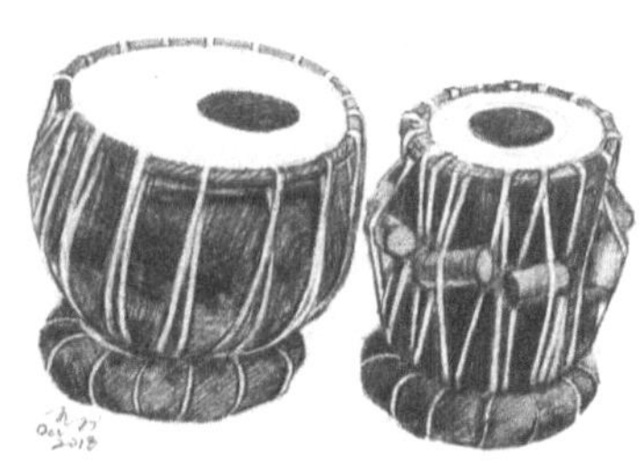

The Holy Koran (Quran)

It consists of a compilation of the verbal revelations given to the Holy Prophet Muhammad over twenty-three years. The Holy Koran is the Holy Book or the Scriptures of the Muslims. It lays down for them the law, commandments, and codes for their social and moral behavior and contains a comprehensive religious philosophy.

The Hydrological Cycle of Water

It is the continuous process by which water is circulated throughout the earth and the atmosphere through evaporation, condensation, precipitation, and the transpiration of plants and animals; also called *'hydrologic cycle.'*

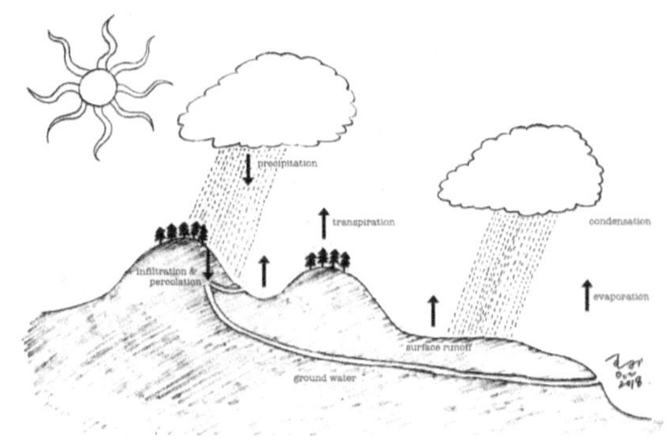

Torus

These are traditional water holes used throughout the deserts of Baluchistan and Sindh Provinces of Pakistan.

Tubas

This is a traditional water hole in rural areas of the deserts. The water can last for months on end. But when it dries-up the people have to move is search of another water-hole to survive.

Our Fathers' Fate Press Release
Perth, Australia (PRWEB), 12 November 2015

Author Sean McQuade brings readers into an unforgettable journey through the pages of his new book *Our Fathers' Fate* (published by Xlibris AU). In this account of his adventures or misadventures, he lets them witness his travels to difficult parts of countries amidst wars and conflicts. It also includes great descriptions of people, culture, and places.

McQuade has not only seen his fair share of the world but also has experienced it personally. In this travel memoir, he shares this wealth of experience—an unforgettable journey that helped mould him into the man he is today. Readers will discover fabulous hospitable times he spent submerged in cultures. They will also visualize the magnificent places and enjoy the humorous and sad events that accrued in his life's journey—a part of his past, present, and future. According to him, he has fallen into the magical cycle of *Our Fathers' Fate* and has become a spoke in the wheel of the cycle of life.

An excerpt from the book's introduction: There were many people in the countries I was in who were facing the reality of having members of their families killed on a daily basis. Their very existence was a never-ending challenge, and they were in dangerous situations that evolved at a moment's notice. It amazed me as to how God could let all this suffering happens to so many innocent men, women, and children.

An engaging and informative read, *Our Fathers' Fate* imparts to readers a better understanding about local communities in many parts of the world through one remarkable man's life journey.

OUR FATHER'S FATE
Sean McQuade
Hardcover | 6 × 9 in | 284 pages | ISBN 9781503505919
Softcover | 6 × 9 in | 284 pages | ISBN 9781503505902
E-Book | 284 pages | ISBN 9781503505896
Available at Amazon, Barnes & Noble, and many other online bookstores.

Xlibris Publishing Australia, an Author Solutions LLC imprint, is a self-publishing services provider dedicated to serving Australian authors. By focusing on the needs of creative writers and artists and adopting the latest print-on-demand publishing technology and strategies, we provide expert publishing services with direct and personal access to quality publication in hardcover, trade paperback, custom leather-bound and full-color formats. To date, Xlibris has helped publish more than 60,000 titles. For more information, visit www.xlibrispublishing.com.au or call 1800 455 039 to receive a free publishing guide.

Follow us @XlibrisAus on Twitter.

Related Reading Links

Murders, rapes, and killings India 1947;
https://www.dawn.com/news/1169309

Slave kids forced to ride races in UAE;
https://www.gluckman.com/camelracing.html

Child labourers exposed in Pakistan;
https://borgenproject.org/child-labor-in-pakistan-2/

Perform ablutions after eating camel meats;
https://islamqa.info/en/answers/7103/eating-camel-meat-breaks-wudoo146

Massacres in Kashmir 1947;
https://countercurrents.org/2016/11/1947-muslim-massacre-in-jammu

The Kamoke Massacre 1947;
https://www.sikhiwiki.org/index.php/THE_KAMOKE_MASSACRE

Modern day slavery Pakistan;
1. https://dailytimes.com.pk/101599/bonded-labour-in-pakistan-a-humanitarian-crisis/
2. https://www.huffingtonpost.co.uk/richard-cw-miller/child-labour-pakistan_b_4694541.html

Lord Mountbatten;
https://en.m.wikipedia.org/wiki/Louis_Mountbatten,_1st_Earl_
Mountbatten_of_Burma

Japanese attack india from Burma in 1947;
https://www.reddit.com/r/history/comments/28t9xe/in_june_of_
1944_japan_attacked_india_from_burma/

Grand Trunk Road;
https://en.m.wikipedia.org/wiki/Grand_Trunk_Road

History of Bridges in India an Pakistan;
https://www.indianetzone.com/38/history_indian_bridges.htm

History of Faletti Hotel Lahore;
https://www.falettishotel.com/history

Tribes of Sindh Province Pakistan;
https://casteinpakistan.blogspot.com/p/sindhi-tribes.html

What it was like to live in India 1900 to 1947;
https://www.quora.com/What-was-it-like-to-live-in-India-during-1900-
to-1947-before-independence

Thousands of Boys Trapped as Camel Riders and Jockeys

Every year, some hundreds—perhaps thousands—of boys are trafficked from Pakistan and other impoverished communities, mostly Muslim countries, to the Middle East where they are forced to work as camel jockeys.

Human rights activists say the boys are treated like virtual slaves: beaten, starved, often crippled, and then discarded when they cannot do the task any longer.

The best camel jockeys are usually small and lightweight. So when race organizers visit Pakistan, looking for riders, they target the youngest children they can manipulate.

Child advocates here say boys as young as two and a half have been taken to oil-rich Gulf States in the Middle East.

Today an estimated 40,000 child jockeys are riding in races in countries such as Oman, Kuwait, Qatar, and the United Arab Emirates.

Most of the boys come from poor families and are taken from mostly Muslim countries, such as Pakistan, Bangladesh, and Sri Lanka.

There are human rights organizations and NGOs in Pakistan working with former child jockeys.

They stated in a lot of cases that kidnappers grab the boys off the street then smuggle them out of the country.

Other times, well-dressed men approach poor families, offering them charity.

Some of these kidnappers, when approaching poor children's parents, pose as rich men and [say,] 'I want to sponsor some of the children' or 'I want to give your children an education and good future'. But in this case, a good education means learning how to race camels.

The children sleep in metal huts and rise at dawn to start their training. The young jockeys are strapped into their saddles to keep them from slipping off the charging animals which weigh over 400 kilograms, more than 10 times as much as their tiny passengers. The camel's approach speeds up to 40 kilometres an hour. Accidents are common.

'Sometimes they fall off the camels and the camels run over their bodies,' he said. 'You will see every second or third boy with a broken arm or broken leg.'

The children also endure more lasting injuries. The constant friction and bouncing of the saddles cause kidney damage and, in some cases, impotence.

To keep the riders' weight down, the boys are underfed before major races. And according to the United Nations, children considered too heavy to race are often abandoned to join the region's growing underclass of undocumented workers.

A London-based advocacy group Anti-Slavery International says the boys who do make it out describe the racing camps as virtual prisons.

'They talk about being beaten if they don't win the races. They talk about not having enough to eat, not having time off.'

Many boys are never paid or are paid far less than their parents were promised.

For years, international aid organizations have pressured Middle Eastern governments to end the use of children in camel races.

Most Gulf States do have laws banning the practice. Generally, children under the age of 15 are barred from riding. Rules are usually ignored at private racetracks in the region.

'This is a sport that many influential and powerful people take pleasure in, and so there clearly isn't a real will to do something about it in terms of prosecuting offenders under existing regulations.'

But things may be changing. The United Arab Emirates has just signed an agreement with the United Nations, pledging action against child traffickers.

UNICEF, the UN's children fund, stated there are around 4,000 child jockeys in the Emirates.

Under the new pact, the UAE promises to reinforce an existing ban against using children in camel races.

UNICEF's Gulf States regional representative in a statement said; the government has compiled lists of all the camel clubs and farms in the Emirates.

For the first time, she says the government appears committed to protecting underage jockeys.

'And they are planning to crackdown and go after the farmers and actually search for the children,' she said.

She says the UAE has also agreed with UNICEF to establish two rehabilitation centres for former child jockeys. Doctors and social workers will help the children recover until they can be repatriated and reunited with their families.

Assistance will continue even after the boys go home, with extra funds promised for education and social services.

The government also announced plans to replace the children with lightweight robot jockeys.

Prototypes have been successfully tested and officials say they hope the first batch will hit the tracks later this year.

Almost Tomorrow Characters

<u>Mrs De Souza</u>

Parveen's mother and Mushtaq's mother-in-law. She was the great-grandmother of Sani, Neela, Imran and Caleb who disappeared in Kamoke.

<u>Mr Sanjay</u>

Parveen's father and Mushtaq's father-in-law. He was the great-grandfather of Sani, Neela, Imran, and Caleb.

<u>Mr Michael De Souza</u>

Killed while fighting the Japanese army in Northern India in 1944. Prior to that, he was the stationmaster in a lay missionary in Goa.

<u>Parveen</u>

Mushtaq's mother and the grandma of the four children Sani, Neela, Imran, and Caleb.

<u>The Malik</u>

Mushtaq's illegitimate father. He was married into an arranged marriage with another woman and was a father of twin sons.

<u>Asahi</u>

The wife of Mushtaq, the daughter-in-law of Parveen, and the mother of four children Sani, Neela, Imran, and Caleb.

<u>Tariq</u>

A kidnapped boy from Deri Ghazi Khan District, Pakistan.

<u>Mr and Mrs Edward and Mavis Braganza:</u>

The owners of Fayette's Hotel in Lahore City. The hotel was nationalized along with several missionary schools and hospitals. Edward later became an 'Honorary Portuguese Consulate General' soon after partition. The Braganza family moved to a humble townhouse in the suburbs of Lahore City and continued to serve the community and social networks providing guidance to the needy.

<u>Mr Tom and Marilyn</u>

English couple living in Fayette's Hotel. While in Pakistan, they resided in Fayette's Hotel, Mall Road, Lahore. Mr. Tom was an alcoholic with a lust for fortune and never married Marilyn. They both disappeared around the time of partition (1947) and rumored to have gone back to England on one of the many merchant navy ships.

About the Book

Even though this book *Almost Tomorrow* is fictional, it is based upon the life story of an Anglo-Indian lady from Goa pre-partition of India oriented around 1947 and, there afterwards, includes tales of the lives of her extended family.

Parveen and her younger sister Bulbul had, through no fault of their own, ended up trapped for life as bonded laborers in the brick-kiln industry in Pakistan.

Their drama began at an early age when their family moved from Goa to a small railway town called Kamoke situated in rural Punjab. The years just after World War 2, with the partition of the Indian subcontinent and the formation of Pakistan and India as separate independent nations, came into being. An account of one single massacre in the Kamoke railway station provides the reader with a window into what might possibly have happened to a portion of approximately 1.5 million people who were murdered or killed during the mayhem.

Also, that year, the mighty British Raj was preparing to finalize their occupation of the Indian subcontinent and return to Great Britain. They had repulsed a Japanese massive attempt to invade Northeast India from Burma. The British army, along with the support of a couple of Indian regiments and American air support, suppressed the advance.

One of Lord Louis Mountbatten's chief contribution was to coordinate the partition on behalf of Her Majesty Queen Elizabeth. He also was responsible for drawing up the new international (Radcliffe Line) boundary between the two new countries. The agreement went ahead on the 14–15

August 1947 in the company of Prime Minister Nehru representing India and Jinnah, the 'Quaid-E-Azam' (Founder of the Nation), representing Pakistan.

Back Cover Notes

band; as per OUR FATHERS' FATE
India - Pakistan - Indian Subcontinent Pre-partition 1947 - India - Pakistan

Parveen and her younger sister Bulbul had, through no fault of their own, ended up trapped for life as bonded laborers in the brick-kiln industry in Pakistan.

Their drama began at an early age when their family moved from Goa to a small railway town called Kamoke situated in rural Punjab. The years just after World War 2, with the partition of the Indian subcontinent and the formation of Pakistan and India as separate independent nations, came into being. An account of one single massacre in the Kamoke railway station provides the reader with a window into what might possibly have happened to a portion of approximately 1.5 million people who were murdered or killed during the mayhem.

Also, that year, the mighty British Raj was preparing to finalize their occupation of the Indian subcontinent and return to Great Britain. They had repulsed a Japanese massive attempt to invade Northeast India from Burma. The British army, along with the support of a couple of Indian regiments and American air support, suppressed the advance.

One of Lord Louis Mountbatten's chief contribution was to coordinate the partition on behalf of Her Majesty Queen Elizabeth. He also was responsible for drawing up the new international (Radcliffe Line) boundary between the two new countries. The agreement went ahead on the 14–15 August 1947 in the company of Prime Minister Nehru representing India and Jinnah, the 'Quaid-E-Azam' (Founder of the Nation), representing Pakistan.

The story began in the 1980s. Praveen, at the time was a grandmother, shared her stories with a group of workers at the end of their hard day's work in the clay pits, brick kiln, and farmlands.

As the sun sank low in the skies, out across the semi-arid desert, one could not but notice how, at forty-eight, Parveen looked much older than her age because of the harsh climate and her individual lifelong struggle for survival. Nothing much had changed in their lives since she and Bulbul were transported to live in the desert. This was where they learnt to face up to the various issues because of inadequate health facilities, and lack of basic infrastructure. Regular droughts, famines, infant mortality, malaria, and waterborne diseases were commonplace reality.

Unlike the Sahara Desert, the Thar Desert areas consist mostly of barren outreaches of non-productive lands and sand dunes covered with thorny short bushes and clumps of wild grasses. In most cases, the unhospitable ridges that are topped off by the most amazing sand dunes with their irregular shapes and sizes and roughly paralleled closed contours have sheltered valleys hidden deep in between. Some of the larger dunes tower overhead in heights of up to fifty metres or more. Whenever it rains, the valleys become wet enough to grow rain-fed crop cultivation, and when not cultivated, they yield an abundance of one-metre-high grasses. Many local inhabitants use these grasses for constructing of traditional-style roof materials or screening compound fences that provide privacy for the extended families living within. The salinity of the subsoil and shortage of portable water makes it hard to sustain a healthy lifestyle for both man and beast alike. But even so, one can't but admire this majestic terrain that is rather picturesque in its own setting. Life goes on, and generations of Sindhi families continue to endure and scratch out existence from the desert.

Parveen carried the burden of the disappearance of her eight-year-old grandson who disappeared at the church Christmas celebrations. However, Imran and his new-found friend Tariq were supposedly kidnapped by a syndicate of people smugglers before they had been shipped off overseas to the United Arab Emirates to participate in wild camel races to entertain the wealthier elements of that society and the international expatriate community. The kidnappers spent eight months training the boys and a few other kids in the art of camel riding, camel racing, and basic Arabic and Middle Eastern customs.

Special thanks Sushi Owaki from Japan for his clasic imaginary illustrations that match perfectly!